DETECTIVE IN THE FAMILY

DETECTIVE IN THE FAMILY

by

F. L. CORNISH

VICTORY PRESS
EASTBOURNE

Printed in Great Britain for
VICTORY PRESS (Evangelical Publishers Ltd.),
Lottbridge Drove, Eastbourne, Sussex,
by Richard Clay (The Chaucer Press) Ltd.,
Bungay, Suffolk.

CONTENTS

CHAPTER ONE

THE PHOTOGRAPH

Grandpa Harris was dozing in his rocking-chair by the kitchen fire. His glasses were perched crookedly on the end of his nose, and his newspaper was spread across his knee, but Paul wondered how fast asleep he really was! Sometimes when you thought Grandpa was asleep you found that he had one eye half open, and was watching you all the time.

Quietly, Paul slid off his chair, and took a few steps across the room. The house was old, and some of the floor-boards creaked very loudly, and you had to walk as carefully as a cat if you didn't want to make a sound. Being small and slight for his ten years, he often managed to get to the other side of the room in absolute silence, and this time he guessed from Grandpa's deep breathing that he had been successful again.

It was not that Paul planned any mischief, but he hoped to become a detective one day, and thought he might as well begin to practise moving silently so that he would be able to catch many thieves, single-handed, when he grew up.

Having successfully reached the big, old-fashioned dresser, he looked around for something interesting to investigate. There was a weather-house with a fat old farmer, wearing a shiny black rain-coat, standing by the door marked WET; and at the other door, marked DRY, stood his wife, wearing a yellow sun-bonnet and a large white apron. Paul swung them gently in and out. On the next shelf, just within reach, were two carved wooden bullocks, and he played with these for a while; but as the minutes ticked by, he looked up at the third shelf, and wondered what was up there. He would have to climb a chair to reach it. Very carefully he drew up a chair, holding his breath as it scraped the floor, but Grandpa still slept.

There were six china plates standing at the back of the shelf, with scenes from Japan painted on them; and then Paul caught sight of a gleam of silver. Standing on tip-toe he could see that it was a photo frame, lying face-downwards on the shelf. Why was it there, and not standing upright on the piano as the other silver frames were? Paul reached up for it, his curiosity making him forget to be cautious, and as he picked up the silver frame he knocked against a small copper jug, and sent it clattering to the floor.

Grandpa Harris woke up with a start, and said in a very sharp voice:

"What are you doing up there, boy?"

"I was only looking, Grandpa," said Paul, nervously, the silver frame in his hand.

"Seems to me you've been doing more than looking. What's that in your hand?"

Paul looked at it.

"It's a photograph of a man, Grandpa," he said.

It was a handsome face, bright and smiling, with thick hair that waved from a wide forehead; a friendly face that would be pleasant to meet at any time, with eyes that smiled back at you.

Paul glanced from the picture to his grandfather, and was quite alarmed to see an angry scowl on his face, and the usually mild eyes glaring fiercely at him.

"Put that down at once, Paul! You have no business to meddle with things."

Paul put down the silver frame where he had found it, and climbed down from the chair, feeling guilty and crestfallen. He stood with his hands in his pockets and his head down.

"Sorry, Grandpa," he murmured.

There was no reply, and when Paul looked up he saw that the anger had left his grandfather's face, and it was full of a dreadful sadness.

Paul's dark eyes were instantly full of sympathy.

"Is he dead, Grandpa?" he asked softly.

"Eh? Dead? How should I know? He's been gone these seven years, and never a word. Your uncle Frank is dead to me, anyway, no matter where he is. I won't have his name mentioned in my house! Now, Paul, it's time you went home. Don't look so worried, lad; its no concern of yours. You just behave yourself, and don't meddle with things. Button your coat up, like Aunt Isobel said; you'll find the March wind blows cold outside."

Paul obediently buttoned up his coat, although his aunt's house was only five minutes' walk away. He walked slowly, his head bent down against the wind, thinking so deeply that he did not see his cousin until she bumped into him.

"You shouldn't walk along with your eyes shut, Paul," she said. "I was coming to fetch you home."

"I don't need fetching," said Paul, irritably. His cousin Emma was all right, as girls go, but she had a superior way of treating him as though he was a very small boy, and she was only eleven herself; 'going on twelve,' she always said. Emma was tall for her age, with long, fair plaits, and blue eyes, and was so good-tempered and easy-going that no one could be cross with her for long.

"You don't look very happy," she said. "Didn't you have a very nice afternoon?"

"Of course I did," replied Paul, kicking a loose stone along the path.

"Emma, who is Uncle Frank?"

Emma tossed one of her plaits over her shoulder, and spoke in her most grown-up way.

"I'm not really supposed to talk about Uncle Frank, but I'll tell you, Paul, because then you'll know why I'm not allowed to talk about him. He was a thief, and he ran away from home, and that's why Grandmother died. Grandpa said she died of shame, but Mummy said her heart was broken."

Paul's eyes were round with wonder.

"What did Uncle Frank steal, Emma?"

"A beautiful ring, made of gold and rubies. Daddy said Uncle Frank probably sold it, because he was always short of money. I was not quite five when he went away, but I remember him. He was my favourite uncle."

They had reached 'Brookside', which was Emma's home, but Paul wanted to ask another question, and kept his hand on the gate as he asked:

"Did they get the police in?"

Emma shook her head. "I don't really know about that; and you'd better not start asking questions either, or you'll be in trouble, and I shall get a scolding for telling you. Come on in, or we'll be late for tea."

'Brookside' was a very pleasant house, with a big, square porch over the front door, and two windows on either side with long, green wooden shutters. The shutters had not been used for many years, and were now partly hidden by creeper, which climbed up from beneath the windows, and looked very attractive when the dark leaves turned from green to fiery red. Mr. John Harris, Emma's father, said the plant ought to be cut down, but nobody had done anything about it. Emma liked to fill her painting book with copies of the leaves in their rich, beautiful colours. Paul liked it, too, because you could nearly always find spiders, and perhaps caterpillars, hidden in the foliage.

In many ways, Paul liked 'Brookside' better than his own home which was in London, and was a very modern flat at the top of a three-storey building. It was equipped with every convenience, including a lift, but it had no garden; not even a window-box to grow anything in. Paul's mother declared that she had no time to begin 'messing about with plants', which was quite true, and was part of the reason why Paul liked to stay with his cousin, and play in the large, untidy garden, where there was plenty of room to dig holes in the soil, and plant apple-pips, or plumstones, or poppy seeds.

Emma rang the bell, and the door was opened by Mrs. Isobel Harris, whom anyone could see, at a glance, was Emma's mother. She had the same fair hair and blue eyes, and was tall and graceful, as Emma would be one day.

"Come along in, children," she said. "Tea has been on the table for five minutes, and you know Daddy likes us to be punctual. Wash your hands quickly, Paul. I have some surprising news for you."

"What is it? Will I be pleased?" asked Paul, standing on tip-toe to hang his coat on the hall-stand, refusing to let Emma hang it up for him.

"I'll tell you about it while we have tea," replied his aunt.

Perhaps this was not a very wise thing to do, because Paul was so excited by the news that he could scarcely eat any tea at all.

"Your mother and your father are both coming to 'Brookside' for the weekend," announced his uncle, while Emma poured out the tea.

"I thought they were going to Italy for a holiday", said Paul, surprised.

"They have changed their plans, dear," Aunt Isobel explained. "They have had to make new plans rather quickly. How would you like to live here with us all the time, Paul, instead of going back to London?"

Paul's heart leapt at the thought, but he said slowly:

"It would be very nice, Aunt Isobel, but I couldn't leave mother on her own in the London flat, could I! Daddy goes away a lot on business, and she would be lonely without me."

Aunt Isobel smiled at him.

"But your mother is coming to live here too."

Paul jumped up so excitedly that he knocked his cup over, and the tea poured on to the tablecloth and splashed the plate of bread and butter just as Emma was taking her first piece. With exclamations of dismay his aunt ran to get a cloth; Uncle John picked up the cup, while Emma rescued the bread and the cakes, and everyone talked at once, and Paul declared that he didn't mean to do it, and it wasn't his fault, and he was very sorry.

When peace was restored again, Uncle John explained that Paul's father had been asked to go on a special mission to New Zealand, and would be away for at least six months, and had decided that it would be better for his wife and son to live at 'Brookside', where they would be with the family, instead of living on their own in London. There would be plenty of room for them in the big house, and Paul's mother could have her own sitting-room.

This news was so tremendous to Paul that it made him feel quite strange. He wanted to ask a hundred questions that came crowding into his head, and yet he wanted to be quite alone and think it all out. Emma was chattering away, but Paul was not even listening.

He was really quite thankful when Aunt Isobel sent him to bed, and the mystery of his uncle Frank was quite forgotten.

CHAPTER TWO

PAUL WANTS TO KNOW

During the next few weeks there was so much cleaning and re-arranging of rooms going on at 'Brookside', that Mr. Harris declared his intention of putting up a tent on the lawn, and camping out until the house had settled down again. Paul and Emma were enthusiastically ready to support him, but Aunt Isobel would not hear of such a thing.

Every weekend Paul's parents drove down from London with the boot of their car filled with personal belongings, and gradually Paul found his bedroom beginning to look like the one he had in London. His own favourite pictures were on the wall; his own desk in the corner, so full of papers and toys and games that the lid would not shut properly. Even his own rug was on the floor; it had been made in the same shape of a bear, and he was extraordinarily fond of it.

Altogether, Paul felt that he was having the best of both houses, and found the arrangement very satisfactory indeed. He was rather sad about not seeing his father for six months, although in actual fact he was used to him going away on business for short periods of time. Even this had its compensations, because Father always sent interesting post-cards of the places he visited, and Paul kept them all in a small filing cabinet. He had been saving post-cards since he was five, and was very proud of his collection, covering nearly every country of the world.

The only drawback to these happy arrangements was that Paul had to join a new school, and that is not always an easy thing to do. The first week was difficult, and he felt lonely and strange, but gradually he made friends with other boys, and by the end of the third week he began to feel that he really belonged to St. Luke's School, and was not just a visitor. He liked Miss Wilson too. She was pretty, with fluffy yellow hair and a gentle smile, except when she was angry, and made you shiver in your seat if you were the guilty one, because her voice could sound like a whip. But it was Miss Wilson who really started Paul thinking again about his uncle Frank. She had been teaching the class about the kings and queens of England, and had drawn a family tree of the royal line of the Tudors.

"Every one," she explained, "has a family tree, even if it is only a small one. Perhaps you would all like to draw one of your own family, and I will give a prize to the one who draws the neatest. If you could find some old photographs, too, that would make it more interesting."

Paul went home determined to win that prize. His family was very small, so it ought to be quite easy to write down their names in the proper order. He talked it over with his mother that evening.

"Miss Wilson said we can begin with our grandfather, or our great-grandfather if we like, but I haven't got one, have I?"

"No, Paul, he died when you were a baby. You had better begin with your grandpa Newman, who is your daddy's father. He had one son, who married me, and then we had you."

Paul chewed the end of his pencil, and looked doubtfully at his mother.

"Where does Emma come in? Isn't she part of my family?"

"Yes, of course she is, but she belongs to the Harris branch of the tree, not the Newmans."

"But isn't Grandpa Harris my grandfather too?" asked Paul, beginning to think this task was not so easy as he had supposed. His mother sighed and picked up the book she had been reading.

"I really haven't time to explain all that, Paul. Go and ask your aunt to sort it out for you; she knows everything about the family history."

Aunt Isobel was much more helpful, and showed Paul how to write the names down in their proper order.

"I think I have a photograph of your mother when she was a little girl, and you could take that to school if you promise not to lose it. I'll get my album down and show it to you."

It was in the family album that Paul saw again the picture of his uncle Frank, and recognised it at once. It seemed to Paul that the bright eyes recognised him, too, although he knew it was only his imagination.

"Who is this, Aunt Isobel?" he asked, hoping she would talk about it.

"That is your uncle Frank," replied his aunt, hurriedly. "Shall we turn over the page now?" But Paul would not be distracted.

"Why haven't I seen him? Where does he live now?" he asked, leaning his arms on the big album.

"He was in trouble, and went away on his own," she replied, in a low voice.

Emma nudged Paul's arm, and frowned at him, but he took no notice.

"Why doesn't he come back, Aunt Isobel?"

His aunt closed the album quickly, and spoke with unusual sharpness.

"Children should not ask impertinent questions. It's time you began to get ready for bed, both of you."

She turned away, putting the album back on its shelf, and the children did not see that there were tears in her eyes.

Emma was most indignant as they went upstairs together.

"I told you, Paul, not to ask questions about uncle Frank," she said. "Now you've gone and upset Mummy. Why don't you just forget about it!"

"I don't want to forget about it," replied Paul, stubbornly; "I want to find out whether he was a real thief, and where he is now."

"I wish I'd never told you," said Emma, crossly. "I didn't know you weren't to be trusted."

Paul's face coloured angrily. "You're horrid to say things like that. I wish I had never come to live with you. Girls are all the same; I hate them!"

Emma tossed her plait over her shoulder and made no reply, and they parted on the landing where they had rooms opposite each other. But Emma could not bear to be bad friends with anyone, and ten minutes later she opened Paul's door. She had brushed her hair, and it hung over her shoulders like a pale gold cloak.

"Can I come in, Paul? I have something for you."

Paul sat on the edge of his bed, moodily digging his bare toes into the carpet. He tried to glare at Emma, but she looked so pretty and nice that he just said, not too graciously:

"What is it?"

"It's a text-card that I got in Sunday school last week for remembering the scripture verse. I thought you would like it because it has a picture of a steam engine on it."

Paul took the card in his hand, admired the engine, and read the words aloud.

" 'Seek and ye shall find.' Find what?" he asked.

Emma hesitated.

"Well—er—find what you are looking for, I suppose."

She had a feeling there was much more meaning in the words than that, but she had never really thought about it before.

"Do you like it, Paul?"

"Yes. Do you think it is true, about seeking and finding?"

Emma was shocked.

"Of course it's true; it's in the Bible. Didn't you know that? Everything in the Bible is true."

A dreamy, thoughtful look came into Paul's dark eyes, and he said slowly:

"Then I am going to do it. I am going to seek for Uncle Frank and find him. But I won't ask anyone in the house, Emma, so don't worry. I shall be like a proper detective, and look for clues. You can be my assistant if you promise not to tell anyone else a word about it, not a single soul."

Emma adored secrets, and even if it seemed a hopeless cause she was quite willing to have a share in it. Her eyes were full of admiration for her cousin, and she forgot for the moment that she was 'going on twelve' and meekly consented to be his assistant.

"All right, put your hand on this card," said Paul, solemnly. "Say, I promise to help find Uncle Frank, and to keep the secret."

Emma promised, and the children parted, the very best of friends. Paul put the card under his pillow, and fell asleep to dream that he was climbing a family tree, and Uncle Frank was right at the top, a long way beyond his reach. In the morning he asked his mother whether dreams always came true.

"Of course not, dear. Sometimes the very opposite thing happens."

Paul was satisfied. Now he would begin the great search for clues.

CHAPTER THREE

A NEW FRIEND

Any boy who wants to become a detective will soon realise that the first lesson he has to learn is patience. A whole week went by without Paul gaining even one crumb of information, being hindered by his promise to Emma not to mention his uncle Frank's name to anyone in the house; but on the following Saturday morning he found an unexpected ally.

It was baking day, and Aunt Isobel had made a batch of Grandpa Harris' favourite spiced buns, and wanted someone to take them along to him. Everyone was busy except Paul, so he volunteered to take them.

"Carry them carefully, Paul, and remember to bring the cake-box back with you. I do wish your grandfather would sell 'Briarcot' and come here to live. It would save me a great deal of trouble, especially when he gets bronchitis and I have to keep running backwards and forwards looking after him. But there, I suppose if you have lived in a house all those years you don't feel you can leave it."

The buns were still warm, and smelled delicious, and Paul hoped his grandpa would give him one. Aunt Isobel did not agree with children eating cakes between meals, but if Grandpa offered him one it would surely not be polite to refuse.

Unfortunately, his grandfather was out. The door was opened by Mrs. Appleby, the lady who came in daily to keep the house clean and cook the mid-day meal. Paul liked her, and thought her name was very suitable, because her face was round and rosy like an apple, and she was a plump, jolly sort of person.

"Come in, Paul," she said. "Mr. Harris will not be back for half an hour, and I shall be glad of a bit of company. Come and sit in the kitchen, and I'll give you a drink of my blackcurrant cordial; there's nothing like it for growing boys!"

Paul gazed at her thoughtfully, as he sipped his cordial and nibbled a ginger biscuit.

"Are you very old, Mrs. Appleby?" he asked suddenly. "I mean have you been here a long time?"

"A good many more years than I like to count, Paul," she said. "I came to this town when your grandmother had her first child, and I was only fifteen at the time. I've worked in this house, on and off, ever since."

Paul sat straight up in his chair, eager to hear more, but remembering his other rebuffs he spoke cautiously.

"Did you know all about my uncles and aunts when they were children, Mrs. Appleby?"

"Of course I did, and a bonnier family you never did see!"

Paul used his most winning tones, and looked at her pleadingly.

"Would you tell me about them, please; especially about my uncles. Were they all good boys?"

Mrs. Appleby laughed merrily, and leaned her arms on the table, putting aside the silver she had been cleaning.

"They were much the same as any other boys, with their good days and their bad days. Edward and John were quiet ones, rather like you. William was always getting into scrapes, but Frank was the wild one."

"What was he like?" asked Paul, eagerly. "Was he wicked?"

"No, indeed he was not wicked," answered Mrs. Appleby, indignantly. "I never knew him to be cruel, or mean, or deceitful, and he could never tell you a lie if he tried. It was just that he liked to have his own way, and was often disobedient, and always being punished for breaking the rules. He was the trial of my life, and yet I think I loved him most of all."

"Did my grandmother love him too?"

"Yes, she did. Even when Frank was naughty he could always win his mother over to his side with his loving, merry ways. He wanted to be a sailor, and twice ran away, and was brought back again. I sometimes wish he had gone to sea, and then all the trouble might not have happened."

Paul slipped off his chair and stood beside her.

"Do you think that Uncle Frank stole that ring?" he asked.

Mrs. Appleby shook her head.

"I am quite sure he never did! Where that ring went to, I don't know, but I will never believe that Frank stole it."

"Were you here when it happened? Can you still remember it?"

"To be sure I can, Paul; it was the night before your grandmother's birthday. She was upstairs in her bedroom, and the dressmaker was finishing the dress she was going to wear for the birthday party. Your grandmother took off her ring before she tried the dress on, in case it should catch in the fine lace that hung from the sleeves, and put it on her dressing-table. Then it was that your uncle Frank came home. He had been gambling, and lost a lot of money, and your grandfather was terribly angry with him. They had a dreadful quarrel! The dressmaker was sent home, and Frank went up to his mother's room. What he said to her we don't know, but the next morning Frank was gone, and the ring was missing."

Paul's dark eyes were almost as troubled as Mrs. Appleby's.

"Perhaps the dressmaker took it," he said.

"No, I'm quite sure she didn't. Janet Megan was a woman you could absolutely trust. She arrived early next morning, and helped me to clear up the bedroom. We searched every corner, and Mrs. Harris turned out every drawer, but there was no sign of the ring. She had to tell Grandfather, and he was very angry and certain that Frank had stolen it."

"And did Uncle Frank never come back?"

"Yes, he came back that night; I think he had remembered it was his mother's birthday. But his father accused him of being a thief, and said many harsh and bitter words, and Frank just walked out again, and no one has seen him since. That was nigh on seven years ago. I'd give anything to know what happened to him."

Paul regarded her very seriously for a moment.

"I am going to look for Uncle Frank," he said. "Only its's a secret between Emma and me. You won't tell anyone, will you! "

"You can trust me, my boy. What makes you think you can ever find him?"

Paul drew from his pocket a rather crumpled text-card, and showed it to her.

"It says. 'Seek and ye shall find', and that is what I'm doing."

Mrs. Appleby smiled, and put her arm round him lovingly.

"I hope you won't be disappointed. You've set your heart on a very big thing, and you are only a little chap, but, if you think I can help you at all, you just come and see me. Mind you, until it is proved that your uncle didn't steal the ring, it wouldn't be any good bringing him home; your grandfather would still keep the door shut against him. He's that proud, he won't forgive his own son! There's your grandfather's step on the porch. He'll be that pleased to see you; and don't forget the buns."

Paul ran home with his mind full of the story he had heard, and he talked it over with Emma at the bottom of the garden.

"We've got to find that ring, Emma. It couldn't have vanished into the air. If Uncle Frank didn't steal it, it must be here somewhere."

Emma was planting sweet-peas in her own flower bed, and was not very encouraging.

"Don't forget, that ring has been lost for seven years, Paul." she said.

"That makes no difference. I've read about people finding treasure that was lost for a hundred years!"

"Well, we can't start looking for it today. Daddy said you can have the piece of ground over by the old apple tree for your garden, only it needs a lot of digging. You can have some of my seeds if you like."

"No thanks," said Paul, as he ran off to find a spade; "I'm going to grow sunflowers."

He had always wanted a patch of ground for his very own, and everything else was forgotten for the moment.

Sometimes he wondered whether he could be a gardener and a detective!

As the days became brighter and warmer, Aunt Isobel began to complain about Grandpa's house. Every year she grumbled about the dreary state of the rooms, and the need to redecorate them, until at last Grandpa had yielded to her insistence, and the date was fixed for the workmen to clean and paint 'Briarcot' from top to bottom. Aunt Isobel went to the house frequently to help Mrs. Appleby prepare the rooms, and Paul and Emma went with her. Their sudden interest in the upheaval puzzled her, and on the second day she spoke to them sharply.

"Whatever has come over you two, always standing around, getting in my way! There's Paul prying into those old boxes again as if he was looking for buried treasure. Now, out you go, both of you, and don't come back here today. Lydia is getting tea for you, as I may be late home."

Lydia was Paul's mother's name.

The children walked slowly out of the house.

"We haven't got a single clue yet, have we?" remarked Emma.

Paul only frowned quite fiercely, and when they reached the gate he climbed over it instead of opening it, for no particular reason. Emma climbed over it after him, but her dress caught on a nail, and there was an awful tearing sound.

"Oh, look!" she cried, in dismay. "This is my second-best crimplene, and Mother will be terribly cross! You don't know how cross she can be, and I'll lose my pocket-money for a week."

"It was an accident," said Paul. "Couldn't a dress-maker mend it?"

"It was your fault," wailed Emma. "If you had opened the gate properly I wouldn't have climbed over. Besides, I don't know any dressmakers."

"Mrs. Appleby does," replied Paul, and then an exciting thought came to him.

"We could go and ask her where that dressmaker lives who made my grandmother's dress, and see if she would mend your dress."

Before Emma could argue about it, Paul ran lightly round to the back of the house, and luckily met Mrs. Appleby as she came to the garden door with a bundle of waste-paper in her arms.

"What a boy you are for questions," she said, in answer to his enquiry. "Janet Megan lives in Birch-wood Road—number 22, I think it is. I haven't seen her for about three months."

"Is it far to walk?"

"About twenty minutes, I should say. What do you want to know for?"

But Paul did not stop to explain.

"I've got the address, Emma," he called, as he reached the gate. "It's in Birchwood Road. Do you know where that is?"

Emma thought hard for a minute.

"I think so," she said slowly; "I think you go over the railway bridge and down a long road to the factory, and Birchwood is at the end of it. Our teacher took us to see the factory last term, that is how I know, but it's an awful long way to walk. Supposing the lady is out! Supposing she is very busy, and doesn't want to see us."

But Paul was not willing to suppose anything, and

his determination overcame Emma's caution, and they set off in the direction of the railway station. It was a long walk, and as they neared the bottle factory the streets became rather narrow and dirty, while the houses were old and neglected. They found number 22, with some difficulty, and stood on the doorstep of the dilapidated, three-storied building, feeling shy, and just a little bit afraid.

"You knock, Emma, because you are the oldest," said Paul. "You say we have come to see Janet Megan."

Emma was not feeling at all grown up at the moment, but she knocked timidly on the door, and was most surprised when it was opened by a girl of about her own age, who stared at her and said nothing.

"We've come to see Janet Megan," said Emma.

"Upstairs," said the girl, and ran off along the dark passage without another word. Paul and Emma stepped inside and closed the door.

"I wish we hadn't come," whispered Emma, but Paul marched boldly up the stairs, and she followed him.

At the top of the stairs a door was partly open, and the children peeped inside. To their surprise it was the brightest, prettiest room you could imagine, with gay cushions and little china figures, and attractive curtains, and flowers in little red pots.

"Good afternoon, children," said a pleasant voice. "Come right in."

They opened the door wide, and there by the window was a lady with the sweetest face and the loveliest smile Emma had ever seen.

Every trace of fear or shyness vanished in an instant.

"I'm Emma Harris, and this is my cousin Paul," said

Emma, her confidence restored; and recollecting that she was 'going on twelve' she added, "I hope this visit is not an inconvenient time", a remark she had often heard visitors make.

Janet Megan laughed softly, and held out her hands to them both.

"It is always convenient to meet friends," she said. "I know you quite well, Emma, although you've grown a lot since I last saw you. Paul I have not seen before, but he is very much like his mother. Now, just make yourselves comfortable, and tell me why you are here."

CHAPTER FOUR

A GREAT DISCOVERY

Janet Megan was small and slight, with black hair and clear grey eyes. She sat on an old-fashioned sofa with a needle-work box beside her, and a piece of embroidery which she put down when the children came in. She did not rise to greet them, and it was not until they said goodbye that they realised she could only walk with the aid of a stick.

"Mrs. Appleby told us where you lived," explained Paul. "We thought you could mend Emma's dress, so that is why we have come."

"It's my second-best dress," added Emma; "Mummy will be so cross with me for tearing it."

"Dear me, you have torn it badly," said Janet, examining it with her capable hands, "but I think we can repair it. Take your dress off, and put this little shawl around your shoulders in case you feel cold."

"Isn't it pretty!" exclaimed Emma, fingering the soft silk. "Where did it come from? Everything in this room is pretty, isn't it!"

"An Indian lady gave me the shawl for making her little girl's dress. I like the things in my room to be gay, especially since I have to spend so much time in here. And how is my friend Mrs. Appleby, Paul? And is Mr. Harris well?"

"They are quite well," said Paul, politely. "My grandpa is going to have his house decorated."

"The rooms are being cleared out already," put in

Emma. "And Paul and me thought we might find— oh!"

Paul had kicked her ankle to remind her not to tell their secret.

"I have not been to 'Briarcot' for a very long time," sighed Janet, and her voice was rather sad. "I expect there have been changes since I was last there, but I haven't forgotten it."

Emma wandered round the room, and stopped before a small, framed sampler that hung on the wall.

"Oh look, Paul," she said in surprise. "This is the same text that I gave you. 'Seek and ye shall find', all done in cross-stitch, with little bunches of violets in the corner. Isn't it lovely! Who made it?"

"My grandmother made it when she was a little girl, and Mother gave it to me when she died. Do you like that text, Emma? You can take it down if you like, and look at it properly."

Emma took it carefully in her hands, and sat beside Janet, looking at it very thoughtfully.

"Do you know what it means?" she asked.

"Yes, of course I do," answered Janet, readily, a smile lighting up her face. "It means that when we are trying to find God, if we seek with all our heart we shall find Him. Many children in this dark world are lost and lonely, not knowing that God has sent His only Son, Jesus to be their Saviour and Shepherd. He loves us all so much that whoever begins to seek shall surely find Him. Even little children can seek and find Him, you know."

Emma gave a little sigh of satisfaction.

"I knew there was a proper meaning to the text,"

she said. "Paul thinks it means if you seek for Grand-mother's lost ring you will find it."

Janet gave a startled gasp, and her grey eyes looked directly at Paul.

"What do you know about the lost ring, Paul?"

It had been in Paul's mind to try to find out something secretly, by asking clever questions, like a real detective, but he did not feel that way at all when he looked into Janet Megan's troubled face.

"Mrs Appleby told me how it was lost, and I thought you might have taken it, but now I can see you are much too nice to do anything bad like that."

Janet's face softened, and tears filled her eyes, though Paul could not tell why.

"Why is it so important to you, Paul, to try and find the ring? Do you want it for yourself?"

"Oh no," cried Paul, who had not even thought of such a thing; "I want to find the ring because—well —you see, if we did find it we would know that my uncle Frank was not a thief, and Grandpa might want him to come back. Nobody knows where he is, but I'm going to look for him. Do you know where he is?"

Janet bent her head over her sewing, and said nothing for what seemed a long while.

"How should I know anything about Frank Harris," she said, at last. "It is nearly seven years since he went away, and I have heard nothing. After all, I was only his mother's dressmaker. It would be wonderful if his name could be cleared of suspicion, so I hope you will go looking for that ring, and if you ever find it will you come and tell me?"

"I'll come as soon as ever I can," said Paul, seriously.

Janet smiled, and the brightness came back into her face. She lifted up Emma's dress.

"There you are, Emma; I've mended it so neatly your mother would hardly notice it had been torn at all. You must tell her about it, of course, and tell her I was very pleased to see you, and to be of help. And Paul, give my regards to your mother. I helped to make her wedding gown, although I was very young at the time. Now you must both go home as my brother will be back soon, and he would be angry if he saw you here. Where's my stick? Ah, here it is. I'll see you to the door."

She rose with difficulty, and walked slowly across the room. Emma's sensitive face was full of sympathy.

"Have you always had to use a stick, Miss Janet?" she asked, gently.

"No, dear, not always. I fell down the stairs, about seven years ago, and hurt my back. Mind how you go down; there is not much light in the hall. Goodbye; thank you for the visit."

The children turned, at the bottom of the stairs, and waved to her before they went out in the street together, and the door closed behind them with a bang.

They had to run almost all the way home so as not to be late for tea, and they both had much to think about. Emma felt that she had made a new and wonderful friend, and was happily resolving to visit her again soon; while Paul was happy, too, quite certain in his mind that no one had stolen that ring—it was simply lost, and one day it would be found.

But there were so many things to do, at home and at

school, and so many other things to think about, that a whole week went by before Paul went to his grandpa's house again. He met Emma after school on Friday, and his dark eyes were shining with pleasure. He held something very carefully in his cupped hands.

"See what I've got, Emma," he said; "I swapped Kevin Jones some Zambian stamps for one of his white mice."

Emma looked at the tiny creature, with its quivering pink nose and ridiculously long tail, and touched it gently with her finger.

"It's no good taking it home, Paul. Mother won't allow mice in the house."

"I'm going to have tea with Grandpa. He'll let me take it in his house. I shall call him Hercules."

"He's too small for a name like that."

"No, he isn't! Anyway, it makes him feel bigger," replied Paul, and, as the mouse was trying to run up inside his coat sleeve, he put it in his coat pocket and held it there.

Grandpa Harris had no objection at all to white mice, as long as they were properly looked after.

"You'll need a warm place where he can build a nest, Paul. There used to be a hamster cage in the garden shed. It's an old one, but it might be just the thing if I can rummage it out for you."

They went into the garden together, and found the cage under a pile of empty wooden boxes. Grandpa looked at it critically.

"The door needs a new catch, and the wire mesh is broken away on one side, but I reckon I can make it as good as new in half an hour."

"Oh, thanks, Grandpa!" said Paul, delightedly. "It

will make Hercules a really new super house. Can we do it now?"

But tea was ready, so Mrs. Appleby found an empty shoe-box, with a lid, and Hercules was installed in it, on a bed of wood shavings, and the lid was secured by a rubber band.

After tea, while his grandfather went into the wood-shed, Paul went to the kitchen to talk to Mrs. Appleby.

"Do you think that cage belonged to my uncle Frank?" he asked.

"No, it would more likely be your uncle Edward's. Frank was too scatter-brained to keep pets; he would forget to feed them."

Paul lifted a corner of the shoe-box to see whether Hercules was hungry, but he was nibbling away contentedly at a diet of crumbled cheese and wood shavings.

"How are the workmen getting on upstairs, Mrs. Appleby?" was his next question.

"They have finished the small bedroom, and I must say it looks a treat, for all your grandpa grumbles about the upset. The men are starting on the big bedroom tomorrow."

"Is that the one where my grandmother slept?"

"Yes, Paul, it was. But you needn't get any ideas into your head about that lost ring. I've swept and washed every inch of that room this week, and it isn't the first time either."

"Can I just go up and see what the workmen are doing?"

"You can if you like, only don't touch the workmen's tools, or fall over the buckets, will you!"

Paul picked up the temporary mouse-cage and went upstairs. The walls were stripped bare, too, and you could see by the cracks in them that it was a very old house.

Hercules was scratching at the lid of his box, and Paul decided to let him out for a bit of exercise; but no sooner was the lid lifted than the mouse ran like a white streak across the table, down one of the trestles, and across the wooden floor.

With a laugh of delight, Paul chased after it, but, although his hand was within an inch of its tail several times, Hercules would not be caught. Close against the wall he ran, and suddenly, to Paul's horror, he disappeared. A small mouse-hole in the wainscoting had offered him a splendid way of escape, and in the twinkling of an eye he was beyond the reach of his owner.

Paul lay flat on the floor, and tried to peer into the hole, but he only got an eyeful of dust. He put his fingers in the hole, but could feel nothing. With a heavy heart he crawled slowly round the room to see if there was another hole that Hercules could come out by, but there was not.

He wondered miserably whether a mouse might starve to death behind the wall. Being a boy, and much too big to cry, he gave vent to his feelings by giving the wainscoting a hearty kick with his strong shoe. There was a sound of splintering wood, and, to his dismay, he saw that a panel of wood had broken away from the wall, bringing down a shower of plaster with it, and leaving a gap where the mouse-hole had been. Paul stooped down, and ran his fingers along the back of the broken wood, and felt among the plaster, but, although there was no sign of the mouse, he felt something soft under his hand. He picked it up, a tiny heap of dirty, mouldering rag; but as he threw it down again, something hard fell out, and rolled on to the floor.

It was something that gleamed and shone as the dust fell away from it. Hardly able to believe his eyes, Paul picked it up.

It was a gold ring, with a single shining ruby in a diamond setting! Paul's face was pale with excitement! So this was what had happened! A mouse, or rat, must have dragged the piece of cloth into its hole to make a nest, and pulled the precious ring along with it.

The next moment Paul was flying downstairs, running out into the garden, shouting for his grandfather.

"Grandpa! Grandpa! I've found the ring! Uncle Frank didn't steal it."

Grandpa Harris was walking towards him, with the hamster cage in his hand.

"Whatever's the matter with you, boy! What are you shouting about!"

Paul had no more breath to explain. He put the ring into his grandfather's hand.

Slowly, the old man dropped the cage, and turned the ring over with his fingers. He looked at Paul, and tried to speak, but his lips trembled, and then he gave a queer, gasping sound and fell to the ground.

Very frightened, and nearly as white as his grandfather, Paul ran back to the house, calling for Mrs. Appleby to come quickly.

"I showed Grandpa the ring and he just dropped down," he cried.

"What ring?" asked Mrs. Appleby as she ran down the garden.

"Grandmother's ring. I found it in a mouse-hole."

There was no time then to ask any more questions. Paul was sent home at top speed to bring Aunt Isobel, and his mother, and to tell them to get a doctor as quickly as possible.

CHAPTER FIVE

MR. JOLLY'S SECRET

The finding of the ring caused great excitement in the family circle, but the rejoicing was mingled with much anxiety and fear for Grandpa Harris.

The shock had brought on a heart attack, and for some days he was very ill indeed, and the children were not allowed to see him.

Paul's mother went to live at 'Briarcot' to nurse him, and Aunt Isobel nearly wore herself out going to and fro, helping in every way possible. Uncle John had taken the ring to his bank, where it had been safely deposited under lock and key, and could not get lost again.

Paul was dreadfully worried and although everyone assured him that he was not to blame, and that Grandpa was very pleased about the ring, he really did wish he had never found it.

At last, one morning Aunt Isobel announced cheerfully that Grandpa was much better, and Paul could go to see him, just for a few minutes.

The sunshine streamed through the window of the bedroom, as Paul walked softly in and stood timidly by the bed, looking down with big solemn eyes at his grandfather. He had never seen him ill and weak before.

"Glad to see you, Paul boy," said the old man, smiling at him. "Don't look so worried; I'm doing fine. I'll be out and about again before the summer's through, mark my words! We've got to get that hamster cage mended yet, haven't we?"

"It's no good now, Grandpa," said Paul. "My mouse never came out of the hole."

"Well, one mouse is as good as another. They always seem to have plenty at the pet shop. If it hadn't been for that mouse, we might never have known where the ring was."

"Are you glad it was found, Grandpa?" asked Paul, anxiously.

"Yes, boy, yes," nodded his grandfather, but he seemed to say it sadly.

Then Paul's mother came in, and the brief visit was over.

It was a great relief when the doctor pronounced Grandfather to be well enough to get out of bed for an hour or so every day. Emma gathered little bunches of flowers for him, from the garden, and Paul brought him news of what was going on at school and at home. Yet, as the weeks went by, the invalid seemed to make no effort to go outdoors, and lost interest in his garden, and even the newspaper failed to hold his attention.

One afternoon Paul called at 'Briarcot' eager to show his grandpa the postcard he had received from his father that day, and as it had been raining heavily, he stood by the garden door, taking his shoes off. He had been walking through puddles in a way that his elders would not approve of at all, and as he stood drying his shoes with his handkerchief, he heard his mother's voice quite plainly. She was talking to Mrs. Appleby.

"If Father doesn't make more effort to eat his food,

Mrs. Appleby, he will never get his strength back. Look at that delicious plaice, scarcely touched."

"What I'm thinking of is this, Miss Lydia," replied Mrs. Appleby. "Mr. Harris is fretting, that's what he's doing."

She never could get used to calling Mrs. Newman by her married name.

"You mean about the ring?" came his mother's anxious voice.

"Well, its plain enough for anyone to see. Now that he knows Mr. Frank didn't steal that ring, he's eating his heart out for the boy to come back. Not wishing to look on the black side, Miss Lydia, but if he don't hear something before the year's out, he'll go down in sorrow to the grave, mark my words!"

"What nonsense you talk!" said Paul's mother sharply. "The doctor said there's no reason at all why he shouldn't recover completely."

Paul seemed not to hear his mother's comment, but Mrs. Appleby's words went straight to his heart. It was perfectly clear to him now: if his uncle Frank was not found, his grandfather would die. That meant there was no time to be lost; he and Emma must think of a plan, immediately.

He was stuffing his wet, muddy handkerchief into his pocket as his mother came out of the kitchen.

"Hallo, Paul, I didn't think you'd come today, in all this rain. Leave your wet shoes here while you go up to see your grandpa. He's feeling a bit tired today, so I shouldn't stay long, dear. Mrs. Appleby is making pancakes for tea."

Paul went slowly up the stairs, and walked softly into his grandfather's room.

The old man lay back in his chair, his eyes closed, his face very thin and pale.

"Grandpa," whispered Paul, "are you awake? Don't worry any more; I'm going to find Uncle Frank."

The blue eyes opened, with a startled glance at Paul.

"Where's Frank? Who mentioned his name? I thought he was here, but I must have been dreaming."

Paul drew close, and spoke earnestly.

"It's me, Grandpa; I mentioned his name. I'm going to find Uncle Frank, because it says on the text, 'Seek and ye shall find.' It must be true, because Emma found it in the Bible. Anyway, I found the ring, didn't I? So now you can eat your dinner, and everything, and get well again. Do you believe me, Grandpa?"

His grandfather took Paul's hand in his, and held it tight for a moment, and a very tender smile softened his face.

"I believe you, Paul my boy. If ever you do find him, tell him his father is waiting; and tell him to hurry. Seven years is a long, long time, and the world is a big place for a man to lose himself in."

"My dad doesn't think so," said Paul, cheerfully. "He says that planes make the world a small place now. They can hop from one country to another like giant grasshoppers, and telephones go round the world, and then there's radio and suchlike. Daddy says you can have supper with a Cairo business man and be in China for breakfast, so Uncle Frank can't be so far away."

Grandfather chuckled, and his eyes twinkled under his heavy brows, making him look like his old self for a minute or two.

"Well now, don't you be hopping across the world, or I'll have to be out looking for both of you! There's your mother calling you down for tea. Ask her if the evening paper has come yet; and what the dickens has she done with my spectacles!"

"Yes, Grandpa," said Paul, and ran lightly down the stairs, wishing he was already grown up and had become a real detective so that he could go out on a big search that very day.

That evening he put the situation before Emma in all its urgency. "We musn't waste any more time, Emma; we must start tomorrow."

"Start where?" asked Emma, who had a practical, down-to-earth way of looking at things.

"At the railway station, of course," said Paul, although the idea had only come to him at that split second. "If I wanted to run away from here I would catch a train that was going as far away as I could get. We could go to the station and see where the trains go to, and that will give us an idea of where a person might go to if he was running away."

Emma, as usual, had a different idea.

"He might have gone away in his car, or on a motor-bike," she said.

But Aunt Isobel settled it after breakfast next morning, which was a Saturday.

"Paul," she said, "I want you to go down to the station for me. Your uncle William has sent some salmon down from Scotland—he thinks it might tempt Grandpa's appetite. It will be in a small fish-basket, so I think you will be able to carry it all right. You can ask the man in the parcels office whether it has arrived."

Emma wanted to go with him, but had to go to a music lesson instead, so Paul set off on his own.

It was a bright, June morning, the air was sweet but cool after the rain, and not many people were about. Those who had to travel to work had gone, and those who were going shopping, or visiting, had not yet started, and no one else seemed to want a train at that time. Paul walked down New Road, and turned left along Railway Street. The station approach was on the right, and you couldn't see it until you were actually standing on the corner. Here a most extraordinary thing happened! Down the slope from the station to the street came a large red hen, running and jumping, wings flapping wildly, and giving forth loud, angry croaks. As Paul stared in astonishment, an elderly railwayman came hurrying out of the station, yelling for all he was worth.

"Susie! Come back! Catch her, somebody! Bother that hen!"

Then Paul did a rather brave thing for a town child. As the hen reached the corner he flung one arm out to clasp her neck, and with the other hand grabbed at her legs. Susie struggled hard, and Paul could only hold her long enough for her owner to catch up with him. He was a short, thick-set man, with a red face and short, stubbly grey hair.

"Give 'er to me, lad," he puffed. "You'd not believe the trouble I've had with this hen today! If you hadn't been there she might have run out to the road and got run over! I'm much obliged to you, boy."

He held the hen fast, in a masterly way, and she became very meek and limp, as if acknowledging that the game was up, while the man went on talking as they walked up to the station.

"I keep a few chickens on my allotment, down there by the sidings, and this morning I brought Susie up to give to a friend of mine coming in on the nine-fifteen, seeing she won't lay much more now. But you'd think that hen knew what was in store for her! Twice she's managed to get away, and that friend hasn't turned up either. I've a mind to put her back in the run, after all."

They reached the station, and the ticket collector, whose name was Mr. Jolly, looked at Paul's coat.

"You need a good brushing down after catching this bundle of feathers, boy. Just wait here till I get back —I'll only be a couple of minutes."

When he came back, he took Paul into his little office, and began to brush the feathers off him.

"Lucky for us there wasn't a train due in. Are you catching the nine forty-five to Overmead?"

"No," said Paul, "I'm not going anywhere. I've come to see if a basket has come for Mr. Harris, from Scotland. Aunt Isobel said it ought to be here on the morning train."

"Ah, you're a bit early for that. The London train don't arrive till two minutes past ten. So you're a Harris, are you? I don't seem to know you though. Been here long?"

"Not very long. Do you know my grandfather?"

Mr. Jolly sat on his high stool, and beamed at Paul.

"Know him? I should just think I did! And those boys of his, why you couldn't help knowing them, lively young shavers, the lot of them."

"They were my uncles," Paul informed him.

"Well, of course they were, you being Lydia Harris' boy. Now you mention it, I can see you've got the family likeness. I heard the old chap—I mean your grandfather—had a nasty turn. Is he better now?"

"Not really; that is, he's better than he was, but he's not well yet. Mr. Jolly, did you know my uncle Frank, the one that went away?"

The smile went from Mr. Jolly's face, and he became suddenly interested in sharpening the pencil that was on his desk.

"Now I wonder what makes you ask about young Frank? I did know him a long time back. Time I got back to work; the Overmead train is due. You can wait on the platform if you like."

Paul watched the local train arrive, and depart, leaving the station quiet and deserted again. He wandered back to the parcels office, and found Mr. Jolly putting special labels on to some large cases. Time was running out, and Paul still had no clues to follow, so he decided to take the bull by the horns, and certainly took Mr. Jolly by surprise.

"Mr. Jolly, when my uncle Frank left here that night, and went away, what place did he book to? Do you remember?"

Mr. Jolly stared at him in great astonishment.

"Do I remember? Do you expect me to remember giving someone a ticket seven years ago? Do you know how many hundreds of people buy tickets at this station every year? Why, I couldn't tell you who bought a ticket here last month, let alone all those years back. You must think I've got a ticket-machine inside my head, young fellow."

All the same, he had not answered the question, and Paul was quick to notice it.

"If you did remember where he went, would you tell me," he persisted.

Mr. Jolly finished his labelling, and stood with his hands in his pockets, looking curiously at Paul.

"What's all this got to do with a little chap like you?" he asked, gently.

Something in the tone of his voice gave Paul confidence. Every detective has to take chances, or he will never find out anything, and Paul was prepared to take a chance that Mr. Jolly was a man to be trusted.

"Mr. Jolly," he said, solemnly, "I have to find out where my uncle Frank went to, or my grandfather will die by the end of the year. Won't you help me to find him, if you can?"

This sounded like something very serious, and Mr. Jolly pursed his lips thoughtfully. He took out his watch and studied it, and put it back before he replied.

"Seems to me a matter so important as that can't be gone into in five minutes. What about coming up and having a chat with me when I come off duty, say about three o'clock? I don't like to think of old Mr. Harris being as low as that! Tell you what—you come up this afternoon, and I'll have some nice fresh eggs for him. You can't beat a nice new-laid egg straight from the nest."

Paul's dark eyes were shining with pleasure.

"I'd like that very much, Mr. Jolly, and so will Grandpa."

"Right! You be here sharp on three and we'll go along to the allotment and talk things over. Wait now, and I'll bring the basket along if it's on the train."

The fish-basket was on the train, and was duly delivered to Paul's care. As he was leaving the station, Paul hesitated, and turned back.

"Mr. Jolly," he said, "I forgot about Emma. She's my partner, you see, and I promised to share with her. Will it be all right if she comes too?"

But at that moment an express train went thundering by, and Paul did not hear Mr. Jolly's reply. He just hoped it would be all right.

Aunt Isobel was pleased to hear about the new-laid eggs, and Emma at once took upon herself the responsibility of collecting them.

"Last time we bought some eggs, Paul, you broke three of them," she reminded him, "so you'd better let me carry them. What else did Mr. Jolly say?"

"Nothing very much," said Paul, airily, but when they were alone he told her that Mr. Jolly knew something about Uncle Frank, and that he was going to help them in their search.

"The only thing is, he might want us to keep it a secret, Emma, so don't you forget that."

Emma shut her lips tight, and made no reply, showing that she was quite able to keep silent when she wanted to, even when she was nearly bursting with curiosity, and that is a very hard thing to do, as every girl knows.

CHAPTER SIX

THE FIRST CLUE

It was with a little feeling of excitement that the children ran up the station approach at precisely three o'clock that afternoon. Paul told his cousin afterwards that he could feel in his bones that something was going to happen; and whether or not this was true, something did happen.

Mr. Jolly smiled broadly when he saw Emma, and commented, as most people did, on the fact that she had shot up like a beanstalk in the last two years.

"I remember the time when you weren't no higher than the door-handle," he said, leading the children out beyond the old railway sidings, and on to the allotments, a narrow piece of ground at the foot of a low embankment. Here there were a few small wooden sheds, and here Mr. Jolly had built his chicken-run enclosed with strong wire-netting.

"Which was the hen that tried to run away, Mr. Jolly?" asked Emma.

"There she is, scratching away in the corner there. That's Susie. She's sulking, I do believe. But we haven't come here to talk chickens, have we! I collected the eggs this morning, and put them in my hut. Come along inside and find yourselves a seat. There isn't much room, but the lady can sit on the stool, and here's a couple of boxes for us men to perch on. The furniture isn't what you'd call luxurious, but I don't generally entertain company, you see."

It was rather dark inside the hut, which had only one small window, and the floor space was mostly taken up with gardening tools, and bags of chicken-feed and a bundle of straw. The air was dusty and warm, and Paul said it smelled like a railway hut.

"I'd like to stay in this hut all day and watch the trains go by," he said.

"Ah, but that's not allowed, this being railway property, though how much longer we shall go on planting our beans here, none of us can say. There's been talk of closing the station down this last two years; and then some say they might rebuild the sidings and use it for freight, so who knows? Meantime I go on collecting eggs, and here's six large brown ones for old Mr. Harris. I'm real sorry to hear about his being so sick."

"Thank you, Mr. Jolly," said Emma, politely. "Mummy says she is sure it will do Grandpa good. She says things taste nicer when a friend gives them to you, but I think eggs taste nice anyway."

Paul was anxious to obtain important information, and his next remark was very much to the point.

"Grandpa will eat all his food when he knows Uncle Frank is found, Mrs. Appleby said, so that's what we've come to ask you about, Mr. Jolly. Are you going to tell us where he went?"

Mr. Jolly ran his fingers through his stubbly hair, making it stand up more than ever, and his face was very serious.

"Well now, supposing I do know, and supposing I tell you, what's to become of me breaking a promise? I promised on oath that I wouldn't tell, and I haven't up to now. It's a mighty solemn thing to break an oath; not to be undertaken lightly, not by any means."

"But if a person is going to die, couldn't you tell then?" asked Paul anxiously.

"I've been thinking, and turning that over in my mind since you asked me those questions this morning, Paul. It may be like splitting hairs, but I did only promise not to tell his parents, or his brothers; I didn't say anything on oath about not telling his nephew, did I?"

Emma agreed with this at once, her blue eyes round and thoughtful.

"You couldn't have, Mr. Jolly, because you didn't know he had a nephew, and Paul was only about three years old then."

"Just what I was saying to myself this morning," nodded their friend, "not that I actually know where your uncle is now, mind you, but I could give you a clue to follow up maybe."

He took a pipe out of his pocket, and knocked on the wooden box with it several times, in silence.

"It was like this," he said, at last. "One night, when the weather was wild and stormy, I came down here after a spell of duty, to see to the chicks. I had half a dozen three-day-old chicks, and two of 'em were sickly, so I came down to see if they were warm enough, and to coax 'em to eat a bit of mash, and here I was when he came striding down the platform, all in the pouring rain."

"Who?" asked Paul. "Do you mean my uncle Frank?"

"Of course; who else should I mean? He came in here, and sat on that very stool, and his face was as white as—as that piece of ribbon on your hair, Emma."

He paused to light his pipe, while Emma twisted her head in an effort to see her ribbon, and Paul sat very tense and still.

" 'I'm in trouble, Jolly,' he says to me, 'bad trouble;' and I could see he was too. He'd been in many a scrape before, but not like this. 'I'm leaving home for good this time,' he said, 'and I don't want anyone to know where I am. My father called me a thief and a liar, and I'll never go back to his house again as long as I live.' 'You'll maybe think better of that one day,' I says to him, but I could see he wasn't in a reasonable frame of mind. 'When's the next train to London?' he says, and I told him there wouldn't be anything till the milk-train went through, about four o'clock. 'That'll do,' he says, and so I let him stay in the hut. I couldn't turn him out into the wind and rain, could I? It was pitch dark too."

Mr. Jolly paused again, but neither of the children spoke, or dared to interrupt the story.

"Well, I made him a cup of cocoa, which I think is very soothing to the nerves, and he told me some of his troubles, which is neither here nor there to you youngsters, and then he handed me a small packet. There's a hundred pounds in there, Jolly, he says to me. I want you to hand this to the person I told you of, and then I'll be free of debt."

"A hundred pounds!" exclaimed Emma. "Where did he get such a lot of money from? You don't think he stole it, do you, Mr. Jolly?"

"No Emma, not he; he weren't that kind of chap. It weren't my business to ask where he got it from either. He told me he had some friends in the fishing business, and he was going to work along with them. I've often wondered how he prospered at sea, him being used to an office, adding up figures all day."

"Did he tell you where the fishing business was?" asked Paul.

"He did, Paul; though he was very much against telling me, and I had to solemnly swear I would not tell his parents, or his brothers and sisters. It was a place called Ferry Winton, somewhere on the east coast, I think. I've still got the name on a piece of paper in my wallet."

"Ferry Winton," repeated Paul, slowly; "I think I've heard that name before."

"Here it is," said Mr. Jolly, taking a small, folded piece of paper from an old leather wallet. "The place was 'Gannet View', Ferry Winton, Wrenshire. But whether Frank Harris stayed there long, or whether he went abroad on one of them Atlantic fishing boats, I wouldn't like to say. I did write a letter to him once, when your grandmother was thought to be dying, but it came back to me after a few weeks. I guess he must have moved on, and I don't know where he is now, no more than anyone else."

Paul jumped to his feet, his face suddenly alight with eagerness.

"Mr. Jolly, you've given us some terrific clues! I'm sure we shall find Uncle Frank now. We shall have to tell Mother and Aunt Isobel about it, but you won't mind, will you? I'll explain to them about you not breaking the oath, and all that, of course!"

"Be careful with those eggs, Emma," said Mr. Jolly, as Emma took hold of the box. "Give my regards to your grandpa, and I'll be looking out for you to come and tell me, if you do get any news."

"We will," promised Emma, giving the ticket collector one of her sweetest smiles, and surprising him by kissing his cheek affectionately. "I think you are a very nice man, Mr. Jolly."

"Aw, come on!" urged Paul, who was rather scornful of his cousin's winning ways. "We've got to get home quickly."

"There's no need to be in such a hurry," protested Emma, when they had said goodbye to Mr. Jolly, and were walking down the station approach. "I can hardly keep up with you, and I've got to carry these eggs carefully."

But Paul was muttering to himself, "Ferry Winton, Ferry Winton; I'm sure I've got a picture of it somewhere."

When they reached home, he ran straight up to his room, and took out his collection of post-cards. It took him a long time to look through them, but at last he found what he wanted.

"I've got it! I've got it, Emma," he shouted, racing down the stairs in his excitement. "Look, it says, 'The old Windmill, Ferry Winton.' I knew I had seen the place before. Daddy sent it to me when I was very small, because of the windmill."

Emma was nearly as excited as Paul, and Aunt Isobel looked at them in surprise.

"What have you two been up to?" she asked. "You look as if you had just discovered a new planet, or something."

"We have discovered where Uncle Frank went to," burst out Paul, although he had intended to keep it a secret until he had explained about Mr. Jolly's solemn promise.

Aunt Isobel's face went quite pale.

"You are not playing a joke on me, are you?" she said, sharply, and Paul looked quite hurt.

"Of course he isn't, Mummy," said Emma, quickly. "You know we wouldn't joke about Uncle Frank. Paul really has found out something about it."

"I'm sorry, Paul dear," said his aunt. "It's just that I feel so anxious about your grandpa that it makes me jumpy. You don't know what it would mean to us all to get news of Uncle Frank. Come into the sitting-room and tell me about it."

So, together, the children told Aunt Isobel the story that Mr. Joly had told them, and she listened gravely to all they had to say.

"Have you ever been to this place?" asked Paul, when they had finished, and he was showing his aunt the post-card.

She nodded, looking at it very carefully.

"We stayed at 'Gannet View' once, for a holiday, but that was a very long time ago, when Frank was a child. This picture is just as I remember it, with the sand-dunes, and the long walk to the sea when the tide was out. There were some crumbling cliffs too, quite low enough for children to climb about and play on. No one was allowed to go very near the windmill, as it was thought to be in danger of collapsing."

"And hasn't Uncle Frank been there since?" asked Paul, looking rather disappointed.

Aunt Isobel thought hard for a moment.

"Now I come to think of it, Paul I believe he did go there again, on his own. He was about seventeen at the time, and was recovering from an illness; I remember his mother saying that the bracing sea-air would do him good. Probably he made friends with some of the people there then."

"And perhaps he's been staying with them all the time," said Emma, dancing about in delight. "All we have to do is to go to Ferry Winton and bring Uncle Frank back home again. Now can we go and tell Grandpa?"

"You just calm down, child, and wait until I have had a talk with your father, and Aunt Lydia, about it. Don't say a word to Grandpa, either of you, until we are more certain of the facts. We don't want to raise his hopes, and then disappoint him, do we?"

Emma heaved a big sigh, but Paul was already thinking how exciting it was going to be to go to Ferry Winton and actually meet his long-lost uncle. It did not occur to him that Emma's father would go without him, and when he heard the next day that Uncle John had already gone there, alone, to make enquiries, he was dreadfully upset. Sad to say, he not only cried, but flew into a temper and shouted at his mother, and banged the door before he shut himself into his room. Emma was astounded and dismayed; she had never seen her cousin in a rage before, but she understood that his disappointment must have been very great to make him behave like that. When he came downstairs an hour or two later, with his eyes red and swollen, and his face very pale, she felt sorry for him.

Paul put his arms about his mother's neck.

"I'm sorry," he whispered, and his mother held him tight, smoothing back his rumpled hair.

"You let that nasty temper get the better of you this time, Paul," she said, gently. "You really must learn to control it, or it will lead you into serious trouble. Now go and wash your face, and come and sit quietly by me, and read your book. Emma can go and feed the guinea-pigs instead of you."

It was really a good thing that Paul was sent to bed early that night, and that both the children were fast asleep when Emma's father returned, because the news that he brought would not have cheered them up at all.

"Not a trace of him, Isobel," he told his wife, sadly. "I made many enquiries, but no one seems to have heard of Frank Harris in that little place. I wonder whether he did go there, after all."

Aunt Isobel made no reply, but suddenly a wonderful idea came into her head, and she told nobody about it until a whole week later.

CHAPTER SEVEN

EMMA HEARS THE TRUTH

It was a lovely Sunday morning, and as Emma ran out of church her face was as bright as the sunshine, and her blue eyes looked as if they had captured two little bits of the blue sky. She tossed her shining yellow hair over her shoulder, and skipped along the street almost bursting with happiness. She had three good reasons for feeling so happy.

That very morning at breakfast time, her mother had announced the astounding news that they were all going to Ferry Winton for a week's holiday as soon as the school term ended. She had written to the people who lived at 'Gannet View', and everything was arranged. Emma could hardly stop thinking about it, even when she was in church.

The second reason was that she had won a golden star for reciting her text correctly every Sunday for three months. That really was quite an achievement, because if you happened to forget one week, or lose your card so that you couldn't learn the words, you had to begin all over again, and not many children won a golden star. Paul had said that Emma could never do it, and now she had proved that she could.

The third reason for this being a specially happy day was that she was going to have lunch with Janet Megan, and that gave her a feeling of being very grown-up, going out to lunch all on her own. She had visited Janet twice with her mother, to be measured

for some summer dresses, and twice with Mrs. Appleby, who liked to share the local news with her friend
when she had time, but this was the first time Emma
had been on her own. She had strict instructions to
leave the house not later than three o'clock.

It was quite a long walk, and as Emma drew nearer
Birchwood Road she was wishing Miss Megan lived at
her end of the town, instead of in these dreary streets.
Yet there must have been a time when they were fresh
and new, and the houses were brightly painted, and all
had pretty curtains at the windows.

She came at last to number 22, and found to her surprise that the front door was partly open. Being hesi-
tant to walk in uninvited, she knocked and waited, but
no one came, and after a few minutes she stepped inside. Seeing no one about she walked slowly up the
stairs, and nearing the top she heard voices; one of
them was a man's voice, speaking in loud, angry tones.

She reached Janet Megan's door, and stood there
listening; not that she meant to be an eavesdropper,
but because she was afraid to go in.

Janet's voice sounded very distressed.

"You must not say such wicked things, Geoffrey;
they are not true."

"I will say what I like," shouted the man. "I say
Frank Harris was a thief, and you had no business to
give him all that money."

"He promised to give it back to me. It was only a
loan."

"You'll never see that money again, and neither will
I. You know I wanted to invest that legacy of yours in a
little scheme that would have brought us both a lot of
money. I don't want you to have anything to do with

that Harris family, I tell you! Don't ever let me find any of them here when I'm at home, that's all!"

Janet's voice replied, but it was too soft to hear what was said. Emma thought quickly; she had no wish to be caught standing there when the door opened, and she was afraid to go down the stairs in case the man ran after her. She looked along the passage, and saw another door, and with her heart beating fast she opened it, stepped into the room, and closed the door behind her. It was a very small room, more like a store cupboard, with a tiny window high up in the wall, and bundles of blankets, and a few wooden boxes on the floor.

Keeping close to the door, Emma waited until she heard Janet's door open and close, and then for one awful moment heavy footsteps came along the passage, stopped by the door, and walked back again, and she heard the man go down the stairs, and the street door shut with a bang.

Very cautiously, Emma went back to Janet's room, and knocked gently on the door. There was quite a long pause before a voice said, "Come in."

Janet was sitting on the settee, and welcomed her visitor with a warm smile, but Emma could see that she had been crying.

"Is it all right to come in? I mean, he has gone, hasn't he? He won't be coming back again, will he?"

"Who? Oh, you mean my brother. No, he won't come back today. How did you know he was here? Did you see him?"

"No," said Emma. "I heard a man talking, so I hid in another room until he went away. I didn't know he was your brother."

Janet looked troubled, but said no more about it then. Emma helped to bring the food in from the kitchen, where it had already been prepared, and sat down to lunch with a good appetite, but her mind would keep going back to the conversation she had overheard. When the meal was ended, and they had settled down for a talk, Emma could not keep her questions to herself any longer.

"Janet," she said, "is it true about that money? Did you give it to my uncle Frank when he went away? And why was your brother so angry?"

Janet's tone was very severe as she replied.

"You should not have listened to private conversation. It is a bad thing to do."

"I couldn't help it, truly I couldn't," explained Emma. "He was shouting, and I was afraid to come in."

"I see," said Janet, but she looked very worried, and walked up and down the room with her stick, before she spoke again.

"I shall just have to trust you, Emma. I did lend the money to Frank Harris. He came to me in such trouble that night, I had to help him, but he promised to give it back to me."

"And hasn't he?" asked Emma, almost wanting to cry herself.

"No, not yet. That is why my brother is so angry. He wanted to borrow the money for some scheme of his own. But no one else knew I had lent Frank the money, and no one must ever know."

"Do you still think he will send the money, after all this time?" asked Emma.

"I still believe in Frank, wherever he is. Sometimes

I think he is like the lost sheep that wandered away from the fold, and I pray every day that the Shepherd will find him, and bring him back again."

Emma's eyes were full of wonder.

"Why, Janet," she said, "that sounds just like my text, the one I had this morning. It said, 'The Son of man is come to seek and to save that which was lost.' Does it mean that Jesus is looking for Uncle Frank too?"

Janet smiled.

"Not exactly, dear; not in the way you are. God already knows where Frank is at this very moment, for He knows all things, but there is another way of being lost. Many people have wandered away from God's kingdom of love and peace, like sheep which have wandered away from the fold, into paths of danger. Jesus, the Good Shepherd, gave His life to save them, and bring the lost ones back to God. This is what your text means."

"I see," said Emma, but she did not really understand. She had never been lost, and did not know that she needed the Good Shepherd to seek and save her, too.

"One thing I want to be sure of," went on Janet. "Will you promise to say nothing about the conversation you overheard? Will you promise to keep my secret, and tell no one?"

Emma's face fell. This was something she simply could not do.

"I'll try, Janet, but I can't be sure not to tell. It's too big to keep inside me, and I know it'll burst out one day when I don't mean to tell. Couldn't I just tell Paul, or Mummy?"

Janet Megan was very understanding, and knew Emma was being honest, and loved her for it.

"All right, Emma. I think the best thing for you to do when you get home is to tell your father all about it. Talk to him when he is alone, and tell him I want no one else to know, and then you can forget all about it. Your father is very wise, and I trust him."

Emma flung her arms about her friend, and hugged her.

"You always say the right things, and I wish you could come to the sea-side with us. Shall I ask Mummy if you can come?"

"That would be fine," laughed Janet. "You and Paul could push me down to the sea in a wheel-chair! No, child—you go and have a lovely holiday, and bring back some sea-shells. Now it is time you went home. If you are going away soon, I shall have to hurry up and finish those dresses for you. Mind how you go down those stairs. Give my love to Paul."

When Emma arrived home, she found her father sitting alone in the garden under the cherry tree, and she was able to tell him all about her visit to Janet, with no one else to hear.

"It was very kind of her to lend that money to Uncle Frank, wasn't it!" she said, at the end.

"Janet Megan is a good woman," replied her father. "Her secret will be safe with me, and with you too. You are not a baby now, Emma, and I want my little girl to grow into a woman who can be trusted."

"I am going to try," said Emma, and she really meant it.

CHAPTER EIGHT

A TALK WITH GRANDPA HARRIS

Aunt Isobel was busy packing, and trying to remember all those things that you have to take on holiday in our English climate, like raincoats and boots in case it is wet, thin dresses and white sandals in case it is hot, and certainly warm cardigans and woollen scarves for cool evenings.

Paul was packing some of his own belongings, and asking questions all the time.

"Can I take my cricket bat and stumps? Why would I need all those pairs of socks? I thought we would be playing on the sand all day in our bare feet. Where have you put my book about sea-shells, Aunt Isobel? I must take that."

His aunt gave a groan of exasperation.

"If you don't stop running in and out and talking non-stop, Paul, I shall never get the job done! It is nearly four o'clock, and I still have a thousand things to do. Why don't you take that guinea-pig down to your grandpa's house, and that will be one item off the list. You'll find an old piece of netting in the shed to wrap him in, and mind you are back here for tea by five o'clock."

"Yes, Aunt," said Paul, running off very willingly to his task. It had been arranged that the guinea-pig should lodge in the old hamster cage while they were away, and Mrs. Appleby had promised to look after him.

"You won't forget to feed him, will you?" Paul asked, anxiously. "He is very fond of cornflakes, and he likes a bit of cheese for his supper."

"I'll treat him like an honoured guest," said Mrs. Appleby. "I only hope he doesn't eat too much, and burst himself before you come back, that's all! My nephew had a guinea-pig that ate too much. They do, you know."

Paul looked worried.

"Well, perhaps you had better give him small meals, and don't let him get too fat. Grandpa said he would keep an eye on him too. Do you think Grandpa is getting better, Mrs. Appleby? He sits in the garden sometimes, doesn't he!"

"Yes, he does, but he doesn't seem to care very much, not even about his roses. When a man like Mr. Harris won't even be bothered to look after his roses, then I say it is a bad sign. But you always seem to cheer him up, Paul. Run along now and have a chat with him before you go."

Grandpa Harris sat in a big armchair by the open window, his hands idly on the arms of the chair, his spectacles perched on the end of his nose, and his eyes almost shut. Paul came into the room with a rush, and stopped himself suddenly, taking a long look at his grandfather, and then silently walking round the room.

When he stood still, by the armchair, his grandfather spoke suddenly, looking at him over the top of his spectacles.

"Well, Detective Inspector Newman, what have you discovered today?"

Paul folded his arms and narrowed his eyes, as he thought an inspector would do.

"Fact one, you have been writing letters; your pen and notepaper are on the table. Fact two, you have walked into the garden, because there is dust on your slippers. Fact three, you have had a visitor, a lady, and she has left her handkerchief under that chair by the piano."

His grandfather laughed, and nodded his head.

"Right every time! I can see you mean to be a first-class detective. You've got to learn to notice little things. Now I suppose you have come to tell me you're going away in the morning; lucky chap you are! What are you going to do with yourself all the week, with nothing there but sea and sand!"

"I can think of a hundred things I want to do, Grandpa," said Paul. "Swimming, and climbing, and looking for crabs, and—well—something else too."

"What else?"

Paul moved nearer his grandpa, and spoke softly.

"I'm going to look for Uncle Frank. Mr. Jolly said—I mean we think Uncle Frank might have gone to Ferry Winton. Did you ever go there, Grandpa?"

"Yes, I did. Your grandmother liked that spot, you know. So did the boys. Paul, open that top drawer in the bureau, and take out a large green folder. Yes, that's right. Bring it to me, and I'll show you something."

Paul handed him the folder, and he pulled out several sheets of drawing paper. These showed delightful sketches of birds, mostly sea-gulls and herons, and little sand-martins.

"Frank did these sketches," said the old man, "and

your grandfather was so proud of them! That boy loved watching the birds, and liked anything that was alive and free. Maybe I was wrong to make him stay in an office, filling in stuffy ledgers."

"He was very clever to draw birds like that," remarked Paul, looking at them admiringly; "I couldn't do it."

Grandpa Harris sighed as he put the drawings away.

"No doubt the boy had some gift with his pencil, but I used to think he was wasting his time. Put the folder back again, lad."

Paul did so, very thoughtfully. There was something on his mind that he had wanted to say for a long time. Perhaps this was the right moment.

"Grandpa," he said, "when are you going to put Uncle Frank's picture on the piano, with all the rest of the family?"

"What picture are you talking about?" said his grandfather, gruffly.

"The one on the dresser. You know, the photo in the silver frame. Only, if Uncle Frank did come back, he might think you didn't want him in the family."

A shadow crossed the old man's face, and his brows drew together angrily for a moment, as pride and sorrow strove together in his heart.

"I can get it for you, Grandpa," said Paul, eagerly, his big brown eyes soft and pleading. "Then you can see it from your chair."

"All right," breathed his grandfather in a whisper.

Paul knew exactly where the photograph was and, standing on a chair in the kitchen, he reached up carefully, and took the silver frame from the shelf.

"I've got it, Grandpa," he said, rather breathlessly,

taking it to him. "Shall I put it on the piano for you?"

"Put it alongside the other boys. That's right. Not that he's ever likely to see it now. Not till I'm dead and gone anyway."

"Oh, Grandpa!" exclaimed Paul. "You know I shall find Uncle Frank soon. You said yourself that I'm a jolly good detective, besides having that text I told you about. Emma said that Janet Megan told her you have to believe in the text or it won't mean anything to you. 'Seek and ye shall find,' the Bible says. Don't you believe what the Bible says, Grandpa?"

"Of course I do," grunted Grandpa, "but I don't see what it's got to do with Uncle Frank. You don't understand it properly."

"Yes I do. It means if we seek God we shall find Him, but I think—well——" Paul could not explain what he meant, and gave up trying. "Anyway," he finished up, "while I am away I shall find out lots of things, and when I come back I shall tell you all about it. I've got to go back now, Grandpa, but I'll send you a postcard."

Old Mr. Harris watched him go, and his eyes turned again and again to the photograph on the piano. He had many things to think about. Did he really believe what the Bible said? He had been to church all his life, but he had never learned to be forgiving, and now he needed forgiveness himself. What did the Book say about that?

That night, when Paul's mother looked into Grandpa's room to make sure he had all he needed, she was surprised to see an open Bible on the table by the bed, and Grandpa looked so quiet and peaceful. She tiptoed out again, without disturbing him.

One other person Paul and Emma had to say good-bye to, and that was their friend Mr. Jolly. He was almost as pleased to hear about the family visiting Ferry Winton as the children were themselves.

"Now you just keep your ears and eyes open," he said to them, "and you may find out something about a certain person."

He nodded his head in a mysterious sort of way, although of course the children knew perfectly well whom he meant.

"I shall be looking out for clues," said Paul. "You never know what might happen when you go on holiday."

"We met a lot of foreigners last year," remarked Emma, "but that was when we went to Southampton, where the big boats come in."

"Talking of foreigners," said Mr. Jolly, "a strange sort of chap came in on the train from London yesterday. There was something about him that made you take notice, though I couldn't put my finger on it, as you might say. He had a short black beard and wore dark glasses."

"Did he speak English?" asked Emma.

"Well, he did and he didn't, if you get my meaning. I suppose you could say he had a foreign accent."

"I expect he was visiting his friends or relations," said Paul. "There's nothing strange about that, is there?"

"Ah, but that's what he didn't do. He asked me if there was a parcels delivery service, and I said there was. Then he gave me a small packet to be delivered to a lady in Birchwood Road. I tried to explain that that wasn't really a job for the railway, but he got a bit upsct and so I told him it would be all right; I'd do it for him privately, especially as he was willing to pay for the delivery. Then what does he do but walk back to the platform and wait half-an-hour for the next train back to London. Now that's what I call strange."

"And did you deliver the packet?" asked Paul.

"Course I did. Twenty-two Birchwood Road, and no thanks I got for it. The man who answered the door was as sour as a bag of crab-apples. I'm a friendly chap and I like to be civil, but since he shut the door in my face I didn't tell him about the foreigner. He can find out for himself if he wants to. But, as I say, you do meet some queer folk. Now you just go and enjoy that holiday, and bring me back a stick of rock. I'm very partial to peppermint rock."

"I shall send you a post-card too," promised Paul, as they went off.

Emma was unusually quiet on the way home. Indeed, she was so thoughtful and absentminded over tea-time that her mother expressed an anxious fear that she was sickening for something. Emma was turning over in her mind the words of Mr. Jolly. She knew that the house where Mr. Jolly had delivered the small parcel was the house where her dear friend Miss Janet Megan lived, and the 'sour' kind of man was probably her brother. Who was the stranger, and what was in the packet?

It was quite wonderful for Emma to have kept these questions to herself, but she remembered her father's words and was really trying to be the sort of person he could trust. After all, it was Janet Megan's concern. She decided to tell her father about it later on. But he was so busy and there were so many things to do, as there always is on the night before a holiday, that Emma forgot to tell him. She forgot the next day, too, and by that time the incident did not seen so important, and it was a long time before Emma even thought of it again.

CHAPTER NINE

A HOLIDAY ADVENTURE

On the first day of the holiday the weather was absolutely perfect. The sea was calm, the little waves
breaking gently on the shore, and the children raced
along the sand, not doing anything in particular, just
enjoying the sunshine, and the clean, salt tang of the
air.

Ferry Winton was a small holiday resort, having
only one hotel, a dozen shops in the narrow main
street, and a few cafés along the short promenade, but
to those who wanted peaceful seclusion it afforded a
pleasant retreat indeed. Westward from the old jetty
the cliffs rose up straight from the sea, but eastward
the coastline sloped down gently to a long flat stretch
of sand-dunes, and here the road turned sharply in-
land to meet wide pastures, and, further in, fruitful
fields of grain.

'Gannet View' was an old house with four bedrooms
on the first floor; above there was a large attic, where
the roof came steeply down to a gabled window.
From here you could see the sea, and hear it, too, on a
rough day.

"I like this room," Emma remarked, on their first
evening at the house. "It makes you feel high up, like
the birds."

"We are high up, very high," said Paul, watching
the graceful sweep of a gull's wing as it glided past the
window. "I expect that was why they called it 'Gannet

View'. Perhaps the people who built it liked watching the birds. Grandpa told me that Uncle Frank liked watching birds, and I expect he stood at this window to get a good view of them."

Emma wandered round the room, examining its contents with great interest. There was a single iron-bedstead in one corner; an old schooldesk with many initials carved roughly on the lid; a broken rocking-chair, and a long, wooden chest that was securely lock-ed.

"Mummy said that she used to play in this room on wet days. I wish the house still belonged to the people who lived here then. Mrs. Barton has only been here two years, and she doesn't know anything about the house."

"It isn't a bad room to play in," agreed Paul, turning away from the window. "We could pretend it was a desert island, and we were shipwrecked on it. I could fix my telescope at the window and watch for a sail on the horizon, and we would have to live on bananas and dog-biscuits."

"You mean ship-biscuits," corrected Emma. "I think I would rather play schools; I like that old desk."

"You could pretend to be teaching the natives to read," suggested Paul, amicably. "But we are not going to have any wet days, so we won't argue about it."

But the next morning the sky was grey, and after one or two light showers the rain set in to a steady drizzle which lasted until the middle of the afternoon. The children were inclined to be quarrelsome, simply because they hated to be cooped up before they had even had time to explore the rocks, or to look for star-fish on the wet sands. Paul was restless, and so touchy that

Aunt Isobel sighed with relief when at last the clouds broke up and the sun shone feebly on the wet pavements.

"It's drying up!" shouted Paul. "Now we can go down to the beach. Come on, Emma; you don't need a coat."

"You can both put your pullovers on," insisted Aunt Isobel, firmly. "You'll find it much cooler after the rain, even though the wind has dropped. Don't go very far, because it will soon be tea-time."

Paul was not really listening, he was so eager to get to the sea. The tide was coming in, and the water glimmered like a pale green pearl where the sun touched it. A light mist was on the horizon, so that you could not tell where the sky and the sea met, and a sudden sense of the wideness and beauty of it all filled Paul's heart with delight. He sat on the edge of a breakwater and took off his sandals, persuading Emma to do the same.

"If we walk out to the edge of the water we might see some jellyfish or a hermit crab. I'll race you across the sand."

"We ought not to go far," remonstrated Emma, but Paul was already out of hearing, and Emma had no intention of being left behind. With her long fair hair flowing out behind her, her bare feet on the cool, wet sand, she ran in the direction of Paul, and then went on running for the sheer joy of it, wishing she could run right on to the end of the world. Then she stopped, breathless and happy, gazing out at the sand-dunes which seemed to stretch out for miles and miles.

Paul caught up with her, holding something in his hands.

"Look what I've found! A hermit crab inside a whelk shell! I wish we had brought a bucket with us to put him in."

" I don't like crabs very much," said Emma, looking at it very dubiously. "I'd rather find some pretty shells. I wonder whether there are any large scallop shells on the beach, or those sort of bluish, razor shells."

"Let's walk along here and see what we can find," suggested Paul. "We could put them in one of those empty ice-cream cartons that you sometimes see lying around. I think I can see one over there. Come on, Emma, we'll only go a little bit further."

The children did not really mean to go so far, but when you are walking along the edge of the sea, with your eyes mostly on the sand, it is very easy to lose a sense of distance, and a sense of time too. An hour can go by, and seem like only ten minutes. Emma and Paul were so engrossed that they did not notice how the sea mist had gradually come shorewards until it was quite near, and appeared to be rapidly closing in around them.

Emma shivered.

"It's getting cold, Paul. We'd better turn back."

"All right," said Paul. "It won't take us long."

But after ten minutes he stopped again, and was less confident.

"I don't like this mist. It's getting thicker, and the tide seems to be coming in very fast. Do you thing we ought to go across the sand-dunes and find the way back by road?"

"Do you know where the road is?" asked Emma, her anxiety growing deeper.

"Not exactly, but I've seen it on the map, so I know there is a road. It would be better than walking into the sea, anyhow."

Emma was begining to feel afraid, but remembering that Paul was younger than herself she tried to sound cheerful.

"I expect you're right, Paul; there must be a road over there somewhere. Let's put our shoes on first though; my feet are frozen!"

She sat on a piece of rock, drying her feet with her handkerchief, and was putting on her sandals, while Paul just stood and watched her.

"Hury up," she said. "Get yours on."

"I can't," said Paul, in a funny sort of voice.

"Why not?"

Emma looked up quickly, and her face fell.

"Oh, Paul! You haven't——"

"Yes, I have," said Paul. "I must have put them down somewhere when I was looking for crabs. We can't go back now."

The thick white mist swirled about them, and the thudding sound of the incoming tide was no longer pleasant to their ears. It was hopeless to think of looking for shoes.

"It's all right, Emma, I can manage without them. Let's get away from here."

Keeping close together, the children scrambled up the sandbank with their backs to the sea, and went forward as quickly as they could, hoping to find a path somewhere between the humps of sand, but they were not making much progress. It is not easy on loose sand, and when the sand gave way to patches of rough soil, and clumps of spiky buckthorn, Paul went slower and slower. Suddenly he gave a sharp cry. Emma turned to him in alarm.

"What's the matter? Are you hurt?"

"I've cut my foot on a stone, I think. Oh, bother, it's bleeding. Have you got a handkerchief, Emma?"

"It is so wet and sandy. Is it a bad cut?"

She knelt down beside Paul and dabbed his foot gently. Fortunately it was not a deep cut, but his feet were getting dreadfully scratched. Try as she would, Emma could not keep the tears back. She was cold and frightened, and as she tied her handkerchief round Paul's foot she did not trust herself to speak.

"That won't stay on," said Paul, crossly. "Can't you do it better than that!"

Emma blinked back the tears at once.

"All right, do it yourself, clever-stick," she replied, just as crossly.

"I wish I had put my socks in my pocket," went on Paul. "They would have been some help."

Without another word Emma took off her socks, and insisted on Paul wearing them. Her shoes were two sizes too large for him, or she would have shared them with him too.

"If only this mist would clear!" remarked Paul, rather desperately. "We should have reached the road by this time. We must just keep on."

But it is very difficult to steer a straight course in a mist, and the children did not realise that they had taken a wrong direction and were going further and further away from Ferry Winton.

Nearly an hour later, when still the waste of sand and scrub seemed to go on for ever, Emma stopped and simply burst into tears.

"We're lost, Paul," she wailed. "We're lost."

Paul was shivering, in spite of his warm pullover, and his legs felt as if they would not carry him one step further, and his foot was painful, but he would not cry.

"There's one thing sure, Emma," he said; "if we're lost, someone will be out looking for us."

"But supposing they don't find us," wept Emma, giving way to despair. "We might die of cold and hunger in the night. No one knows where we are."

There was a long pause, and then Paul said, solemnly:

"Does God know where we are?"

"Of course He does!" replied Emma, trying to dry her eyes with the skirt of her dress.

"Well then, you always ask God to find Uncle Frank, don't you? Why don't you ask Him to find us?"

Emma felt a little bit ashamed. She was the one who had always been to Sunday school, and she should have thought of it before. The words of the text came back to her mind, that the Son of man was come to seek and to save that which was lost. She closed her eyes and clasped her hands together, and in her heart she prayed, Please God, seek and find us now, because we are lost, me and Paul. But she was a bit shy of praying aloud, and wondered what would be the right words to say. Before she could say anything, there was a shout from Paul.

"Look, Emma, there's something over there. It might be a house."

The mist had cleared a little, and they could see the dim outline of a building not many yards further on.

"Oh," breathed Emma, feeling as if God had worked a miracle for them, "we will be found after all."

They discovered the building to be something like an old log cabin, but there was no light within, and, when they banged on the door, no one replied. They walked round it and found another door, but that was locked too.

"Perhaps the people have gone away," said Emma.

"No, they've been here today, I should think," said Paul, peering in at a window. "There's some bread and milk on the table. I wonder if I could open this window; it seems quite loose."

He rattled the frame gently, getting his small fingers round it, and to his great joy it opened easily.

"Come on, Emma, let's go inside."

It seemed dreadful to enter someone else's home through the window, like a burglar, but it was the only thing to do.

They climbed in, and shut the window to keep out the mist. Although they had been out for about four hours, it was not yet dark, which was fortunate, because there was no electricity in the cabin, and they would not have been able to light the big lamp that stood in a corner of the room. It was quite a long room, with a fireplace at one end, and along one wall was a couch, with four blankets neatly folded on it. Paul eyed them thankfully.

"I'm cold, Emma," he said. "I'm cold and tired and hungry. I'm going to have a drop of that milk and a piece of bread, and wrap myself up in some of those blankets."

"Would it be stealing?" asked Emma, doubtfully.

"No, because we are only borrowing it, and when we get home we'll send the people some money for it. The person who lives here wouldn't like to find two children dead of hunger and thirst when they come back, would they?"

Of course, Emma knew there was no such danger hanging over them, but she drank a little milk, and curled herself up in a blanket beside Paul. It was quiet and still outside, and the light began to fade. As Paul got warmer, he became quiet too, and fell asleep from utter weariness.

Emma, huddled in her blanket, sat very still, but was wide awake. She was still frightened, even in this place of refuge. The awful sense of being lost was much filling her mind, and, although she knew her father and mother would be looking everywhere for her, she felt so lonely and helpless. She thought of the story of the lost sheep, and how the Good Shepherd went after it, and brought it home on his shoulder. She was like that lost sheep, she said to herself, and she remembered that Janet Megan had explained that people were lost by wandering away from God into wrong paths, and that the Good Shepherd gave His life for the sheep, to bring them back into the fold. A great longing to be one of His sheep stole into her heart, and tears filled her eyes. Was the Shepherd seeking for her at that moment? Suddenly she knew that He was very near, quite close.

"Lord Jesus," she whispered, "I'm glad that you've found me. I want to be your sheep for always and always, and never to be lost anymore."

No one but the Shepherd heard that little prayer, but His love gathered the lamb into the fold, and all the fear and terror went out of Emma's heart. She knew now that somehow she was safe and loved and secure.

A beautiful smile lit her face, and though it was almost dark, and nothing had changed in the situation, she just felt sure everything was going to be all right.

Then she heard a dog barking, and heavy footsteps approaching. Her heart beat fast as someone turned a key in the lock, and the next moment a bright torchlight was flashed round the room. The dog barked again but was still held on a lead, and Paul sat up in sudden fright, clutching hold of Emma.

"It's all right," she said, clearly. "We were lost, and came in here to shelter. We only had a little drop of milk and some bread, which we will pay you back."

The man seemed too surprised for words, and simply stared at the two wanderers huddled together on the couch. He was slight of build, with dark hair, and a short black beard.

"Well!" he said at last, speaking with a foreign accent. "Well, by all that's wonderful, it's the children, the lost children! Just you keep right where you are till I get the lamp alight. I never am so pleased before in my life!"

CHAPTER TEN

MR. CRUSOE

In the glow of the lamp, the children watched the amazing excitement of the man, who seemed unable to decide what to do first.

"You are cold? You want a hot drink? I will make some coffee—but no, you will want the fire to warm you. Sit down, Lass. Good dog! Now where have I put the matches? I must go and tell the police. No, I will tell Ma Dunken, and she will tell the police."

All the time he was walking up and down the room, the big labrador constantly getting in his way, sensing his excitement.

Paul came slowly down from the couch, his legs feeling stiff, and his feet sore.

"We'd rather go home now," he said. "Has the mist cleared away? Is it far to the road?"

The man looked down at the small, white-faced boy, and shook his head in perplexity.

"Road? No, only the farm. It is perhaps a mile to the farm. I will go quickly, and come back soon. You will be safe with Lass. Come here, Lass."

The dog came, obediently, and the man stooped down, fondling its ears, and whispering in a language that the children did not understand, but evidently the dog understood. It padded softly over to Emma, and placed one paw on her knee.

"Lass will guard you. You are not frightened? No?"

"No, not a bit," said Emma, looking into the man's

face, noticing the kindly eyes, and the gentle mouth, "What is your name? Mine is Emma, and this is my cousin Paul."

He flashed them a quick smile.

"Pleased I am to meet you. My name is Crusoe; that is what they call me—Mr. Crusoe."

Again he spoke to the dog, who thumped the floor with her tail but did not move from Emma's side, and, picking up the torch, he hurried out.

Reassured by the knowledge that they were no longer in danger, Paul began to look about him. There was another door, no doubt leading to another room, but it was locked. There was no tap, water or sink, and only a small camping stove at the far end.

"I don't suppose anyone actually lives here," said Emma. "Perhaps Mr. Crusoe uses it for a sort of beach hut."

"It's an awful long way from the beach, considering the distance we walked," Paul said, but he was mistaken. When they were walking through the mist they had travelled in a half circle, and were much nearer the sea than they realised.

In less time than one would expect, Mr. Crusoe was back, and with him, puffing and blowing with haste, was a short, plump woman, whom he addressed as Ma Dunken.

Not only did Ma Dunken bring a stream of comforting words, but a can of hot milk, and a bag of freshly baked scones. She warmed some water from an enamel jug, and bathed Paul's foot with capable hands, talking all the time.

"Such a stir there has been about the two of you. A police-car has been touring the area, calling at all the houses, and searching the beach huts. The coastguards have been on the look-out, and a rescue team are going to search the cliffs, and all the time, here you were, asleep on Crusoe's couch."

"Not all the time," protested Paul. "We walked for hours and hours. Then Emma said a prayer, and when we opened our eyes there was this house. We could easily have missed it."

"The praise be to God," said Mr. Crusoe fervently, in a low voice.

"The good news will be all over Ferry Winton by this time," Ma Dunken informed them. "My son Benjie set off on his motor-bike the minute Crusoe told us where you were. I daresay your folk will be over here soon."

Suddenly Lass stiffened, and growled.

"They're here now," said Mr. Crusoe, and then he did a curious thing; at least, Paul thought it was odd. He drew a pair of dark glasses from his pocket and put them on, and with a quick movement of his hand pulled a quiff of hair low over his forehead. It made him look quite different, as if he were a much older man.

But there was no time to ask questions. Mr. Harris, and a tall policeman, and Ma Dunken's son Benjie stepped into the room. Emma's father put his arms round her, and hugged her as if he would never let go, and her tears flowed again, but this time for joy and relief, and her father was not ashamed to have tears in his own eyes. Then he put an arm round Paul, too, and held him close.

"We didn't mean to go so far, did we Emma!" Paul began to explain, but Uncle John interrupted him.

"We will save all the explanations until we get

home. We have to walk quite a long way because the lane was too narrow to bring the car any nearer. Where are your shoes, Paul?"

"They got lost," said Emma, answering for him, "and he cut his foot too."

The policeman stepped forward.

"I'll take the lad, sir; he'll be no weight at all. Climb on my back, youngster, and hold tight."

With many expressions of thanks to Mr. Crusoe and Ma Dunken, they set off across the sands. The mist had quite gone, but the night sky was dark with unseen clouds, and the children were glad to reach the warmth and comfort of the car.

Mrs. Harris received them with a mixture of scolding and tears, insisting that they both had a hot bath, because she was sure they would get pneumonia, and declaring that she would not go through the last few hours again for all the tea in China! The following day she gave them both a long and severe lecture, which they could not easily forget.

But that night, being tucked into bed at last with many a loving kiss, Emma whispered to her mother, sleepily:

"It was all right, Mummy, because the Good Shepherd found me, and I'm never going to be a lost sheep again."

And in two minutes she was fast asleep.

In spite of Aunt Isobel's gloomy fears, Paul and Emma were none the worse for their adventure, and when the morning sun shone brightly into their bedrooms they were quite ready to go shell-hunting again.

Emma's father had a different idea.

"I think we'll have a nice tour of the countryside

today," he said, while they were having breakfast. "There is a very ancient church I would like to visit, about ten miles from here. Perhaps we could have lunch at a farmhouse. There are some Roman remains somewhere in the area, I believe, which I am sure would be very interesting to examine. Don't you think that would make a good day's outing, Paul?"

"Yes, thank you, Uncle John," said Paul, without enthusiasm, and he exchanged glances with Emma. They would much rather have spent the day scrambling among the rocks, but, as Emma explained afterwards, she really owed it to her parents to be extra good and obedient after the fright they had had yesterday. She knew, without being told, that they would not want herself, or Paul, to be out of their sight the whole day long.

Rather to their surprise, the outing proved to be a very pleasant one. Paul found some very attractive post-cards; and in a village shop which sold almost everything you could think of, Emma found a picture of a shepherd with a lamb on his shoulder, in an old-fashioned gilt frame. Her mother was surprised that she preferred the picture to a pretty Japanese doll in a green silk kimono which the shop-keeper tried to sell her.

"You can never tell with children," she murmured to her husband, shaking her head as though she gave them up as a mystery.

On the way home they made a detour, driving into Ferry Winton from the west, to show Paul and Emma how far they had wandered in the mist.

Uncle John stopped the car at a place where the road ran parallel with the sea, and pointed out a small cottage, and a few outhouses, about a mile from the road, almost on the edge of the sand-dunes.

"That is where Mrs. Dunken lives. It is only a small farm, just a few acres of pasture, some cows, and a flock of sheep. Mr. Dunken was a lifeboat man, and was lost at sea in a terrible storm they had here about four years ago. Mrs. Dunken keeps bees, and sells the honey, and her son Benjie looks after the cattle."

"Does Mr. Crusoe live there too?" asked Paul. "Or does he live in that cabin?"

"He lodges at the farm, but I think he spends most of his time in the hut. I couldn't get much information about him."

"I can't see the cabin, Daddy, can you?" asked Emma.

"Not from here. There is a track that leads to it from the farm, towards the sea. I wonder why it was built out there?"

"It's time we moved on, John," said his wife; "I did say we would be home at five."

That evening Paul and Emma were busily writing their post-cards. At least, Paul was busy; Emma was nibbling the end of her pen, and tracing patterns on the carpet with her toe. She never could think what to put on post-cards.

"Who are you sending one to, Paul?" she asked.

"I've written one to Grandpa, one to Mother, and one to Mrs. Appleby. I'll send this one to Mr. Jolly."

The mention of Mr. Jolly stirred a thought that had been at the back of Emma's mind since yesterday, when they had first seen Mr. Crusoe.

"Isn't it funny, Paul," she said; "Mr. Jolly told us about a foreign sort of man with a black beard, and now we've met one too. But the one Mr. Jolly saw had dark glasses."

Paul put down his pen and stared at her.

"This one had dark glasses. Didn't you see Mr. Crusoe put them on just before the policeman came in?"

"No, I didn't notice. That seems very odd, being two of them, doesn't it."

All Paul's detective instincts came to life at once, and his dark eyes shone with excitement.

"I don't believe there are two men, Emma. I think it's the same man. Mr. Crusoe knows Mr. Jolly, and Janet Megan, and he lives at Ferry Winton where Uncle Frank came. Perhaps he knows where Uncle Frank is now! We'll have to go back to that cabin again."

"Mummy said we are not to go there on our own again," Emma reminded him.

"But we must find a way to see Mr. Crusoe. We'll have to think of something! I'm going to tell Mr. Jolly about it."

That was how Mr. Jolly received a post-card that made him shake his head, being completely mystified.

Dear Mr. Jolly,

I hope you are well. The foreign man is here. He has a dog and glasses. He was kind to us, but I think this is a clue. We like this place very much. Best wishes,

Paul Newman.

CHAPTER ELEVEN

ANOTHER CLUE

The postman arrived early at 'Gannet View,' but Emma was already at the gate looking out for him. There was a letter for Paul, and one for her parents. The news from 'Briarcot' must have been a little disturbing, because her mother read it in silence, and passed it to her father, without the comments she usually made.

Emma's quick eyes saw the worried look on her mother's face.

"Is Grandpa all right?" she asked.

"Yes, he's all right," replied her mother, but she did not sound very sure.

Paul confided in Emma that he had received a letter from Mrs. Appleby, telling him that the guinea-pig was fine and healthy.

"She says she hopes we are having a nice holiday, and have we found any clues yet?"

"What does she mean?" asked Emma, who was not listening properly, being disappointed because she had not received any letters.

"About Uncle Frank, of course, stupid," replied Paul. "I wish Aunt Isobel would let me go to see Mr. Crusoe. I'm sure I could find out something from him."

"You are not to bother Mummy," said Emma, primly. "She is worried about Grandpa, and Daddy is busy writing important letters."

Paul sighed. He wondered whether he could get a lift on the milk-van that called at Dunken's farm every day, but there would be the problem of getting back. Just as he was beginning to feel desperate, Aunt Isobel herself came to the rescue.

She came into the house just before tea-time, and talked excitedly to Uncle John, who was lazily reading some magazines.

"I have been having a long discussion with old Mrs. Murphy at the greengrocers. She told me that her husband had a weak heart for years, and the only thing that brought him through was honey, pure honey. She said some doctor in America had discovered this treatment, and it works wonders! I told her about Grandpa, and she advised me to get some honey at once. She said Mrs. Dunken's honey is the best in the country, and couldn't be improved upon. We must get some at once, John, and send it to him."

"I'll get some tomorrow," said Emma's father. He had been swimming with Emma, and was not used to so much exercise.

"I really think you should go now," insisted Aunt Isobel. "We could send it by first post tomorrow."

Uncle John stood up, with a very resigned air.

"I can't think a few days would make any difference, myself," he said, "but I'll go. Anyone want to come with me?"

In one bound, Paul was at his side.

"I'll come, Uncle John. I'd love to come. What about Emma?"

Emma had been drying her hair, but was just as eager to go.

When they arrived at Mrs. Dunken's cottage, she

was busy picking raspberries, but gave them a very cheery welcome.

"Come right in, Mr. Harris," she said. "I hope those children have not been causing you any more trouble. I must say they look a bit brighter than when I last set eyes on them. Is there something I can do for you?"

Mr. Harris began to explain about his wife's urgent request for honey, and Paul, bursting with impatience, asked if they could see Mr. Crusoe.

"He'll be down at the cabin," said Mrs. Dunken.

"Can we go there to see him?" pleaded Emma, but her father shook his head.

"No, my dear, it would take far too long."

Mrs. Dunken had a tender heart, and when she saw the great disappointment on the children's faces she made a bright suggestion.

"If my Benjie could spare the time to take them down there, they could have a bit of tea with me, and maybe you could call back for them in an hour or two. How would that do?"

The children thought it would do splendidly, and Emma's father could seldom resist the appeal of her lovely blue eyes, especially when her mother was not there to be firm.

"All right," he said, "I'll be back at seven o'clock, only no wandering off across the sand on your own!"

This assurance was readily given, and the children went off to find Benjie, who, his mother said, was on the other side of the yard, mending the fence.

He gave them a slow, shy smile, and went on repairing the fence, which took him about another ten minutes. He was not usually a talkative young man, but

Paul kept up such a barrage of questions that in the end he got what he called 'quite wound up,' and talked all the way to the cabin.

"Who built that cabin?" asked Paul, as they set out over the sand-dunes.

"My grandfather."

"Why did he build it there?"

"He was an ornithologist."

"I know what that means," Emma put in. "It means the study of birds. I know, because there is a book about it in the attic at 'Gannet View,' and Daddy told me what it meant."

"That's right," said Benjie, smiling at her, "grandfather built it so as he could watch the birds. There's some fine sea birds to be seen in these parts—terns and cormorants, and the great black-backed gulls."

"Does Mr. Crusoe watch the birds?" asked Paul.

"Sometimes."

"Has he lived here a long time?"

"No, only since the storm. That will be four years ago come mid-summer."

"That was when your father was lost at sea, wasn't it," said Emma, slipping her hand into Benjie's large one, by way of expressing her sympathy. "It must have been a very bad storm."

"Worse than ever I saw before or since."

"Did Mr. Crusoe come in the storm?"

"Well, since you seem so interested I'll tell you how it happened," said Benjie, standing still and pointing out to sea. "I don't suppose you can see the marker-buoy out there, west of Ferry Winton? You'd see it after dark, when the light flashes. Before the night of the storm there was no buoy there, as no one knew about the submerged rocks until the ship was wrecked."

"A real shipwreck?" asked Paul, wide-eyed.

"Real enough to lose five good seamen. It was a day I shall never forget; a hot, still day. The air was so close towards evening that you felt you couldn't breathe; not agrass moved, even the gulls were quiet. Then the sky began to go dull, and lightning began to flash over the horizon. I met my pal Charlie going up to the coastguard station, and he said he didn't like the look of it a bit. It was still as hot as an oven, and then the thunder began to rumble, and the sea started to lift and swell as if it was getting angry about something. All of a sudden it seemed the storm was on us. Pitch black it was, and the rain coming down in bucketsful! Then, about an hour before midnight, it happened; the rockets went up, and the lifeboat crew were called out. A ship was being lashed to pieces out there, blown off course like a matchbox by the power of the storm."

Benjie paused for a moment, and for once Paul was silent, his imagination gripped by it all.

"She was a 'packet', from The Hague, an old ship, doing her last season, and that was the end of her. Four of her crew were lost, and so was my father. But that is how it goes with seamen. My grandfather died at sea too. That's why Ma taught me to love the land, and care for the sheep. She don't want to lose me too, not that way."

They walked along in silence for a while, and then Paul said:

"What about Mr. Crusoe?"

"Ah, yes! I was going to tell you about him. Well,

there happened to be a man up at Ferry Winton, Scott they called him, and on the night of the storm he was on the beach when the rescued men came in. He brought the news up to us, about my father, along with the minister, and then he walked out past the cabin, down to the sand, although he couldn't tell you what it was made him do that at two o'clock in the morning. By that time the clouds were breaking up, and suddenly he heard a crying coming from the sea. He raced down to the water's edge, and could just see something being tossed about in the waves. Then he heard that cry for help again, and being a strong swimmer himself he just plunged straight in, and managed to reach the drowning man who had been clinging to some driftwood. Scott was about at the end of his strength by this time as they reached the safety of the beach, I can tell you. It was an hour later that he staggered into the farm, and after that we managed to get the fellow along to the cabin and dry him out. The next day he seemed to have recovered, but nothing would make him leave the cabin. He couldn't speak much English, and refused to give us his name, so Scott called him Robinson Crusoe, because he had been rescued from drowning, and that is what we have all called him ever since. He calls himself Mr. Crusoe."

Paul asked whether Mr. Scott was still in Ferry Winton.

"He comes and goes," said Benjie. "And there's the cabin."

He gave a low, peculiar whistle, and from the cabin came Lass with such a rush that she almost knocked Paul over, and ran round Emma in boisterous delight.

Mr. Crusoe was pleased to see the children, inviting

them into the cabin, and explaining that although he was very busy he could spare a few moments to give them greeting, and to enquire after their health.

Inside the cabin, they noticed at once that the door which had been locked before was now open, and the little room beyond was full of light.

"Is that where you watch the birds?" asked Paul, eagerly.

Mr. Crusoe smiled, and shook his head.

"I do not watch birds. I am too busy. Mr. Scott watches them. You may come and see, but you must not touch things."

The room had large, glass panels along two walls, giving a clear view of sea and sky and sand. There were a few shelves in the room, containing books on bird lore, and a bench covered with pieces of wood and various small tools.

Emma, forgetting the injunction not to touch things, picked up a narrow piece of wood that was beautifully stained and polished, and decorated with carved leaves.

"Isn't this pretty," she said. "Did you make it, Mr. Crusoe?"

"Yes, it is my work," he said, pleased at her admiration. "I make many picture frames, and models, and sell them. Do you like this one I make for my friend Scott?"

He held up a carving of a wild duck in flight, a very beautiful piece of craftsmanship, and he was evidently proud of it.

Paul was more interested in the man than in his work.

"Who is Mr. Scott?" he asked. "Is he a sailor?"

"Scott is my very good friend. He pull me out of the sea, and call me Crusoe."

"Where is he now? Will he come back soon?" asked Paul.

"Perhaps. I do not know," answered Crusoe, shortly.

He looked at Paul suspiciously, but Paul was gazing thoughtfully out to sea.

"Mr. Crusoe, do you know a man called Mr. Jolly? He is the ticket collector at the railway station where I'm living now. Have you ever been there?"

This time the man frowned heavily, and a look of fear, or anger, crossed his face.

"No. I know not. You ask too any questions. It is bad to ask so many questions. I think you should go away now."

Paul turned round so quickly at the sharp tones in the man's voice that he knocked over some papers that were on the edge of the bench, and they scattered all over the floor.

"I'm sorry," he said, stooping to gather them up, noticing that they were mostly sketches of birds. The last one he held in his hand for a moment, staring at it in surprise. Where had he seen one exactly like that before?

"Give it to me, please," said Mr. Crusoe.

"I know! I remember now," said Paul, excitedly. "It was in——"

But he was interrupted by Mr. Crusoe, who seemed extremely anxious for them to leave the cabin immediately.

"You must go now. I am very busy."

As they walked back to the farm, Emma was quite cross with Paul for having made Mr. Crusoe angry.

"You shouldn't have asked so many questions, Paul. I think it was quite rude of you. Now he won't let us go there again."

At any other time Paul would have begun an argument in his own defence, but all he said was:

"Emma, I've made a discovery! That drawing of a bird is exactly the same as the one Grandpa showed me. It was one of Uncle Frank's drawings of a sea-gull flying, I'm absolutely sure. But how did it get here? Do you think Mr. Crusoe knows Uncle Frank?"

Emma was very doubtful. "Lots of those bird pictures look the same," she said. "It might have been drawn by someone else."

But Paul was confident that he had found an important clue in his search for a lost uncle, and, like a good detective, was determined to follow it up.

CHAPTER TWELVE

SEEKING AND FINDING

The next two days were so full and happy, with special treats, including a trip out to sea in a motor-boat, that Paul had no opportunity of finding out anything more about Mr. Crusoe, although he thought about him very often.

On the third morning something happened that made Paul feel as though a big black cloud had suddenly spread across the sky. Early in the morning there was a telephone call for Emma's father, and immediately afterwards he ran up the stairs, calling anxiously:

"Isobel, it's bad news! Grandpa has had a relapse and is seriously ill. Lydia thinks I should be with him. We must go home at once."

Paul could hear Aunt Isobel's calm voice answering him.

"Now don't get panicky, John. Lydia may have let herself get frightened; you know how she worries about things. I think the best plan is for you to drive straight off after breakfast, leaving me and the children here until you find out what the situation really is. I can begin packing, and if it is really necessary the children and I will return home by train. Phone me as soon as you can!"

It was a damp, drizzly morning, and Paul and Emma watched at the window as the car drew out of the drive and went swiftly down the road.

Paul was very worried indeed. An anxious fear was growing in his mind. Supposing Grandpa was to die before Uncle Frank was found! It was a dreadful thought, and made Paul feel that he must go and see Mr. Crusoe at once.

"Emma, we've got to go to the cabin, or to Mrs. Dunken's farm, now."

"We can't, Paul. You know Mummy said we were not to go there on our own."

"I'm going to ask her again then. If she knows how important it is she will let us go."

But Aunt Isobel would not listen to Paul's explanation. She was too busy packing, and sorting out clothes.

"Don't bother me now, Paul, there's a good boy. No, you may certainly not go to the farm on your own, and I haven't time to take you. Go upstairs and get your things together, just in case we have to catch a train in a hurry."

Paul went slowly up the stairs to the attic, where Emma was putting her particular treasures in a small case.

She could see at once that Paul had not received permission to go to see Mr. Crusoe, by the gloom on his face.

"I told you Mummy wouldn't let you go," she said. "It's no use sulking about it."

This was just the sort of remark that could be counted on to make Paul feel worse. His temper began to rise.

"I suppose you don't care, Emma, if Grandpa never sees Uncle Frank again." He picked up Emma's shepherd picture that was lying on the desk.

"That's not true! Anyway, you haven't found him yet. Where's my picture? Give it to me, Paul."

She held out her hand, but a sudden spitefulness took hold of Paul.

"I won't," he said.

Emma made a grab at it, and Paul flung the picture across the room, where it hit the wooden chest, and fell, smashed and broken, to the floor.

Emma gave a cry of dismay. "Oh, my lovely picture! You hateful, beastly boy, I shall never speak to you again!"

She burst into tears, and Paul, his face red with anger, ran down the stairs, and out of the house.

It was still raining slightly, but he did not care. He did not care about anything or anyone, and rebellious thoughts chased each other through his mind. He was not sorry for Emma; it was her own fault. He hated Aunt Isobel, and told himself that she was cruel and unjust. With hands thrust deep in his pockets, and head down, he walked on and on. The tide was far out and the beach almost deserted as he walked towards the sand-dunes. Then he thought he heard someone shouting to him, so he began to run, determined not to turn back for anybody. Suddenly he tripped over some big stones and fell flat on his face. He was not hurt, but lay just as he had fallen, and felt himself to be the most miserable and ill-used boy in the whole world! He started to cry, big, choking sobs, and could not stop. Of course he knew, deep down inside him, that his own bad temper was the real cause of his misery. He loved Emma, and had not meant to be so unkind, and now she would never speak to him again.

He thought of his Grandpa, too, and wished he could see him, and talk to him. Presently he felt something touching his head, pushing gently against him, trying to lick his face, and he sat up to see the big body of Lass the labrador standing over him. A few feet away, Mr. Crusoe stood looking down at him; he was not wearing the dark glasses, and his face seemed to be shining with happiness, making him look so different that Paul wondered whether he really was the same man.

"So, we meet again! You are the boy who wants to know all the answers. This time I will ask the questions, and you will tell me the answers. Why do you lie on the wet sand and cry? Did somebody beat you?"

His voice was kind and friendly, and Paul was so lonely and sad that it was hard to keep back the tears. He looked at Mr. Crusoe with dark, tragic eyes, and his lips trembled. This was his opportunity to ask straight out all about this mysterious man, but all he said was:

"I lost my temper."

Mr. Crusoe sat down on the sand beside Paul and offered him a clean white handkerchief to dry his wet face and brimming eyes.

"Ah, this temper, it is a bad thing. I do not care about it until I go to prison, then I care very much."

"You went to prison?" exclaimed Paul in surprise, forgetting his own distress for a moment.

"I did. They all say, he has a bad temper; he killed his father. So they put me in prison."

"And did you kill your father?" cried Paul, aghast at the thought.

"No, I did not kill, but everybody knows I have bad temper, and when I am in prison I think and think about this. How can I get this temper out of my heart? I do not know any way at all."

Paul sighed, sympathetically. He had often wished there was some way of getting rid of his quick temper.

"Then the little child came to the prison with bread for us, and she talks about the good Word of God that she learns in the school. I do not laugh at her, as some do, and she tells me that Jesus will give me a new heart, and take away the bad one. I think about this for a long time, until she comes again, and I ask her how do I get this new heart, and she says, 'Ask Him, if you are sorry for your bad temper, and then it will be done.' It is a miracle, I said; and it was too."

"And did the bad temper go away at once?" asked Paul, deeply interested.

The man smiled at him, and spread out his hands expressively.

"It was ten feet high, it was six feet high, it was two feet high, and it was so small I put it under my thumb, like this."

Paul stroked Lass's head thoughtfully, and enquired, without looking up:

"Do you think that could happen to me?"

"If you want to get rid of the temper, yes. It is like getting out of prison, and being free."

Paul decided there and then that he would ask Jesus to give him a new heart too, but he wanted to do that when he was by himself, so all he said was:

"How did you get out of prison?"

Mr. Crusoe dropped his voice and whispered:

"I escaped! I hid in a cave on the mountain, then I make my way to the coast."

This was a thrilling adventure, and Paul listened eagerly.

"There I waited my chance," went on Mr. Crusoe. "There, at night I see the packet-ship, and while it is dark I climb on board, and I hide."

"You mean as a stowaway?"

"That is what I do, and it is very dangerous and uncomfortable. Then the storm comes, the big storm, and the ship breaks. I have never been to sea before, and am terrible fearful. I cling to a piece of wood, and try to swim away. I am nearly drowned when I call for help, and my friend Scott hear me, and rescue me. I have never seen him before, but I owe him my life. All that I have I will share with him."

"But won't they be searching for you?" asked Paul, looking out to sea as though he expected the police to appear over the horizon at any minute.

Mr. Crusoe laughed, and jumped to his feet.

"They cannot hurt me now. I am done with hiding and disguising! My friend Scott has brought the papers to prove I am innocent, and I am free; only yesterday he brings them, and today I am so happy, so happy."

"Where is Mr. Scott now? I would like to ask him something."

"He is in the cabin. Come! You shall meet him."

Paul scrambled to his feet, and took Mr. Crusoe's hand.

"That is not your real name, is it, Mr. Crusoe?"

"It is not, but I like it."

They were not far from the cabin, and Paul's heart

beat with a strange sort of excitement as they approached it. Perhaps this Mr. Scott had actually met his uncle Frank, and might even know his whereabouts!

As they entered the door, a man came from the inner room, and looked at them in surprise.

"Hallo," he said, in a very pleasant voice. "I wasn't expecting visitors."

Paul saw a tall man, sunburnt and brown as a gipsy, with even his moustache bleached fair, and his hair at the temples showing almost platinum against the dark skin. He had an open, friendly face, with merry blue eyes that won an answering smile even from Paul's woe-begone face.

"This is Paul, the boy that was lost," explained Mr. Crusoe. "I bring him because he wants to meet you. He always asks questions."

"Then I suggest we have a nice cup of coffee together, and I'll see whether I can give him the answers. Put your coat over that chair, Paul; it looks very damp to me. Now, while Crusoe makes the coffee we'll have a chat. Ask away!"

The smile faded from Paul's face as his anxieties came rushing back into his mind, and he fixed his serious dark eyes on Mr. Scott.

"Do you know anything about my uncle Frank?"

The man looked startled for a fleeting moment, and asked quickly:

"Frank who?"

"My uncle, Frank Harris. If you know anything about him, please help me to bring him back. Grandpa is dreadfully ill, and I'm so afraid he'll die if I can't find my uncle. I've been looking for ages!"

Mr. Scott rose suddenly and walked over to the window, and then came back and sat down, close to Paul.

"Look here, old chap, why don't you begin at the beginning and tell me the whole story. I meet a lot of people in my travels, and I might be able to help you."

So Paul told him all that had happened, how it had begun by him finding the photograph. He told about the text, 'Seek and ye shall find,' and how he had found the ring, and how Grandpa had been taken ill. He spoke of his friend Mr. Jolly, the ticket-collector, and how he had mentioned Ferry Winton, about the holiday at 'Gannet View', and how he had met Mr. Crusoe.

All the time Paul was speaking, Mr. Scott sat with his hand shading his face, and said not a word. When Paul had finished his story, he asked, still without moving or looking at him:

"What makes you think I can help you?"

"Because of the bird-drawing that is in that room. Mr. Crusoe said it was yours, but I think you must have got it from Uncle Frank, because I'm sure it is the same one."

At that moment, Lass, who all this time had been sitting motionless at Mr. Scott's feet, growled softly in her throat, head up, and ears well back.

"Someone is outside," said Mr. Crusoe, but strangely enough no one moved; they all looked towards the door, which had been left partly open, as though they were waiting for someone who was expected.

Suddenly the light flooded in, and Emma stood before them. The sun had just broken through the cloud, and shone upon her yellow hair, turning it to gold, and she seemed tall and graceful, framed in the doorway, her cheeks so pink, and her eyes bright blue.

The man called Mr. Scott sprang to his feet, and they heard him catch his breath.

"Isobel," he whispered.

Emma gave him a brief smile. "No, I'm Emma," she said, and turned to Paul. "Oh, Paul, why did you run away? Mummy was so upset, but I told her I could find you, and so I have! But we've got to go home at once, because of Grandpa."

Paul scarcely heard what Emma was saying. He was looking at Mr. Scott, whose face was almost pale under the suntan, and whose expression as he gazed at Emma was very strange indeed. Suddenly the man turned and looked at Paul, and in a flash Paul grasped the truth.

"Uncle Frank!" he cried out. "Uncle Frank! It was you all the time! Your name isn't Scott at all."

"Yes, it is. Frank Scott Harris is my name, and I am your uncle!"

Paul gave a shout of joy.

"Then I have found you! Emma, the text did come true; I have found him!"

Emma's eyes were round with wonder and amazement.

Frank Harris sat down, and drew the two children to his side, still with that strange look on his face, as though he thought this was some kind of dream and was not really happening.

It was Emma who broke the spell, in her practical way.

"Uncle Frank, we have to go back now. Mummy said if we miss the train we might be too late."

Uncle Frank seemed to wake up with quite alarming suddenness and vigour. He spoke to Mr. Crusoe in rapid German, rushed about collecting his things, hurried out of the cabin and across the sand dunes towards the lane so fast that Paul and Emma had to run to keep up with him.

A small grey car was in the lane.

"Jump in, both of you," said Uncle Frank, breathlessly. "I'm going home."

The car shot away, and the children held each other's hand in speechless excitement. Uncle Frank was found at last!

CHAPTER THIRTEEN

HOME AT LAST

The small grey car drew up at 'Gannet View', and there was Mrs. Harris at the door, looking so worried and anxious.

"Wherever have you been?" she called out, as the children ran towards her. "If only you knew——" She broke off, seeing a stranger behind them.

"I found Paul, Mummy," said Emma. "And we've found someone else too."

Frank Harris smiled, and held out his hand.

"It's me, Isobel. You haven't changed a bit in seven years."

Isobel Harris's face went from white to red, and to white again, as she stared at him.

"Frank!" she said, at last. "Frank! It can't be you!"

"It is me, without a shadow of doubt. Paul has been telling me that my father is ill."

"He is desperately ill. John has just telephoned to tell me that we must get home as soon as we can. I can't imagine how you have suddenly arrived here, but you could not have come at a more opportune time."

"Isobel, can we leave all explanations until another time, and just get going. How soon can you be ready? Where are your cases? What about a few sandwiches for the children, and some coffee; it is a long way back, and we don't want to lose time."

For concentrated activity, thought Paul, no one was going to beat his uncle Frank. In less time than anyone would have thought possible the cases were in the boot; hats, coats, bags and food were in the car; Aunt Isobel shut the door of 'Gannet View', and ehey were all safely started on their long journey.

Paul was simply bursting to ask a thousand questions, but when Uncle Frank said very firmly, "No questions, please", you knew it was not the time to ask anything.

Emma did not seem to want to talk, either, and sat behind Uncle Frank, staring at the back of his head as though she feared he might disappear again. As the miles slid swiftly past, Paul went back in his mind over the events of the day. He remembered his bad temper, and how unkind he had been, and took a side-long glance at Emma, sitting quietly beside him with a brown-paper bag on her knee. He guessed it was the broken picture, by the careful way she had been holding it.

Although he wanted to say he was sorry for what had happened, Paul found it very difficult to put his feelings into words. If Emma had only continued to be horrid to him he would not have felt so bad, but she had not mentioned the incident again.

The car gave a sudden jolt over a bump in the road, and the parcel slipped off Emma's knee. Quick as a flash, Paul picked it up.

"I'm sorry about the picture, Emma," he said. "I was a beast."

"It's all right, Paul," she replied. "I was angry too, after you'd gone. If only it hadn't been my picture; I wouldn't have minded so much about anything else."

Paul looked puzzled.

"What makes that picture so special?" he asked. "It isn't really valuable, is it?"

Emma opened the brown-paper bag and drew out the picture of the shepherd and the lamb. Her mother had carefully removed all the broken glass, and, although the gilt frame was bent, the painting itself had only received a slight scratch.

"It is special to me, Paul, because it reminds me of the Good Shepherd, and how He went out and found the lost lamb. You know when *we* were lost—well, I remembered about us all being lost in sin, and I wanted the Shepherd to find me, and He did, and now I belong to Him for ever. That's why I love this picture so much. I was going to hang it over my bed, until you—until it got broken."

When he began to understand just what that picture meant to Emma, Paul wished with all his heart that he had not broken it. He began to see for the first time that one moment's ill-temper could bring hours of unhappiness to someone else; and then he thought about Mr. Crusoe, and the trouble his bad temper had caused him. Without doubt the safest thing to do was to ask Jesus for a new heart, as Mr. Crusoe had done, and had explained to him when they talked together on the sand.

"I'll save up my pocket-money and buy you a new frame for it, Emma, if you like. Or shall we ask Mr. Crusoe to make one for it; you know what lovely carvings he can do. I like him now. Shall I tell you what he told me this morning?"

"Is it a secret?" asked Emma, her eyes lighting up.

"Yes, in a way it is." Paul lowered his voice to a whisper. "Mr. Crusoe has escaped from prison!"

Emma's horrified expression was very satisfying, and Paul let the news sink in for a few moments.

"Is he a very wicked man?" she asked, in the same whisper. "Are the police after him?"

"No, he's not wicked," replied Paul. "They said he killed his father, but he didn't do it."

"How did he escape?"

"He stowed away on the ship that was wrecked in the storm. Then Mr. Scott—I mean Uncle Frank, rescued him."

Emma gave another adoring glance at her uncle Frank's head, and said with a little sigh:

"Wasn't it brave of him!"

"I think Mr. Crusoe was brave too," said Paul. "I suppose he was afraid of someone recognising him; that is why he wore those dark glasses, and didn't want to meet people. But why should he go to our railway station? That's what I can't understand, even though he said he hadn't been there."

But Emma, not having any ambition to be a detective, was content to let mysteries sort themselves out, being perfectly happy to know that Uncle Frank was found, and they were all going home together.

As they neared the little town of Hunstone, the car began to slacken speed, and they all breathed a sigh of relief.

"We'd better go straight to 'Briarcot'," said Mrs. Harris; "I expect John will be there."

When they stopped at the house, Frank Harris hesitated.

"Do you think Lydia will recognise me? Had you better go in first, and announce my arrival?"

"No, Frank, I want to surprise them. Lydia has seen us already."

Paul watched with great interest the meeting of his uncle with the rest of the family, thinking what strange people grown-ups were, as they all seemed to cry on each other's necks, instead of jumping for joy, but that is how it was. What Paul wanted most of all was to see Grandpa.

His mother put her arms round him tight.

"Darling, I'm so glad you're back. Grandpa keeps asking for you."

"Can I see him?" Uncle Frank pleaded.

"I'm afraid to let him see you, Frank; the shock might be too great."

"But, Mummy! I want——" cried Paul, but his mother interrupted him.

"Be very quiet, dear, and you mustn't talk too much. Grandpa is very ill."

The room was very quiet, and Paul walked softly to the bed where old Mr. Harris was lying propped up by pillows. His face was almost as pale as the sheets, and he looked so frail and ill that Paul wanted to cry.

"Grandpa," he whispered, close to him, "it's me—Paul."

The pale blue eyes opened and looked at him for a moment as if he was a stranger, then they smiled.

"Paul," he said. "You're back!"

"Yes, I'm back, Grandpa. I've got a surprise for you."

The old man looked at Paul with a question in his eyes, looked across the room at the photograph of

Frank in its silver frame, and back again at Paul. He could not speak.

Paul's dark eyes brimmed over with joy and thankfulness.

"Yes, Grandpa, I've found him! Just like it said in the text, 'Seek and ye shall find.' I've brought him back!"

"Where? Where is he?"

"He's downstairs."

A wave of colour swept over his grandfather's face, and left him so white and still that Paul was scared.

"Don't die, Grandpa," he said, in a frightened voice. 'I'll tell him to come now."

"Uncle Frank!" he called out, running down the stairs. "Come quick! Grandpa wants you!"

Frank Harris took the stairs three at a time, and closed the bedroom door behind him.

Paul sat on the bottom stair and burst into tears, showing that he was not very different from the grownups after all. It had been a most exciting day.

Aunt Isobel decided, very firmly, that the children must go straight home to bed, and it was no use protesting. There would be plenty of time to talk to Uncle Frank tomorrow.

To be sure, Paul had to see his guinea-pig first, and Emma had to see how much the flowers in her garden had grown while she had been away; and by the time they had run all over the house to make sure everything was exactly as it had been before the holiday, and had finished their evening meal, it was quite late. Late enough for them to be only just going upstairs to bed when Uncle Frank arrived, to tell them that Grandpa was all right and was sleeping peacefully.

There was a shining happiness in his face as he spoke that reminded Paul of the younger Frank in the photograph. If being a detective always made things come right for people, it would be worthwhile trying to be a good one; but if you were helping to bring a criminal to justice, that would be a different story.

On the following day, the dark cloud gave way to bright sunshine, and everybody felt much happier. Grandpa was pronounced to be out of danger, and, in Mrs. Appleby's words, had 'turned the bend', and would get stronger every day. Much to the children's delight, Uncle Frank came to dinner, and talked to them afterwards, giving a thrilling account of his wanderings, and adventures, and sorrows. He told of how he had first gone to Ferry Winton with anger and bitterness in his heart, and worked for a while with the fishermen, calling himself Scott, but there had not been enough business to support him, so he had joined the deep-sea fishing boats that sailed north to the colder regions. Returning to England, he learned from an old friend that his mother had died, and that made him terribly unhappy. He could not rest anywhere, and went wherever he could find work on a ship, going east or west; it was all the same to him. Then one day, feeling desperately lonely, he turned back to Ferry Winton again.

"I don't know what drew me back," Uncle Frank said, thoughtfully. "It was as though I had to come, and I had only been there three days before the storm. That was when I found poor old Crusoe, as you have already heard. He was so frightened, and friendless, and clung to me like a brother, and I understood him. He had been falsely accused, as I had been. His father had fallen from a narrow ledge on the mountain, and Crusoe had been accused of pushing him to his death, and was imprisoned, awaiting trial, but he escaped. Only one person might have witnessed the accident, and Crusoe begged me to go to Switzerland to try and find him. This needed money, so we worked together, making and framing bird pictures that were sold easily; and as soon as we had enough money I set off on my detective work."

Here Paul interrupted eagerly. "That's just what I want to be, Uncle Frank! Were you a good detective?"

Uncle Frank smiled.

"I don't think I was very good, Paul. One day I'll tell you all about my enquiries. The chief thing was that through the goodness of God I found the man, and the evidence, and Crusoe is going back to his village to fight for his freedom."

Emma gave a sigh of satisfaction. "Isn't it funny," she said; "you were seeking and finding someone, and Paul was seeking and finding you, and the Good Shepherd was seeking and finding me."

A tender look came into Uncle Frank's blue eyes as he looked at Emma.

"I think the Shepherd found me too, Emma, although it took Him a very long time. We'll have a talk about that another day. Now, what about coming to 'Briarcot' with me; your grandfather wants to have another look at you both."

Paul thought that was the end of his investigations, but it was not.

There was still one small mystery to be solved.

CHAPTER FOURTEEN

TROUBLE FOR JANET

Two days later, when Uncle Frank had returned to Ferry Winton to settle some urgent business matters, Emma set out to visit her friend Janet Megan. She had arranged some of her shells very prettily in a little box to give to Janet, and her mind was full of the good tidings she had to tell.

The dingy streets seemed more unattractive than ever, and when she reached number 22, Birchwood Road there was an even more neglected look about the house.

Emma knocked confidently on the door, and it was opened by the girl whom she had seen the first time she went, a girl with a thin, freckled face.

"Hallo," said Emma. "I've come to see Janet Megan again."

"She's upstairs," said the girl. "I'm glad you've come. She's in trouble."

Having said that, the girl turned away down the passage, leaving Emma to climb the stairs, wondering what she meant.

She tapped on Janet Megan's door so gently that Janet did not hear, so Emma turned the handle, and stood inside the room.

What she saw was so unexpected that she just stared and stared.

Gone were the pretty cushions, the dainty covers, and the ornaments. The walls were bare of pictures and the bookshelves empty, the rugs were gone, and only the table, the old-fashioned sofa, and two kitchen chairs were left in the room.

As Emma turned round, Janet Megan came from the kitchen and stood in the doorway, leaning on her stick.

"Why, Emma!" she exclaimed. "This is a nice surprise! I thought you were away on holiday."

"We had to come back early, because of Grandpa," replied Emma. "But what has happened? Are you going away?"

Her face was full of dismay and her voice so tragic, that Janet Megan smiled.

"It's nice to know that someone will miss me. Sit down on the sofa and tell me all about your holiday, and how the family is getting on."

But Emma was too distressed at the thought of losing her friend to talk about herself.

"Why are you going away, Janet?" Then, as a sudden thought struck her: "You're not getting married, are you?"

This time Janet laughed outright, but older eyes than Emma's would have noticed the dark circles under her eyes, the thin, drawn look about her face that told of suffering and sorrow. She spoke quietly.

"No. I have to leave this house. My brother has gone, and I am not able to manage on my own. I have been offered a room at Overmead, for which I must be grateful. Of course I had to part with most of my nice things, but that is just as well. We cling too tightly to such trifles."

Her tone was so sad, in spite of her efforts to be cheerful, that Emma flung her arms round her neck and kissed her lovingly. She could not bear to see her friend in such trouble.

"When are you going?" she asked.

"In the morning. Don't be sad for me, dear; I shall be all right. Now tell me how your grandfather is."

"He is getting better now, but he nearly died. He would have died if Uncle Frank had not come back. We found him at Ferry Winton, after we met Mr. Crusoe."

It was Janet's turn to be amazed.

"Did you say Frank Harris has come back?"

"Yes. He's gone to see his friend Mr. Crusoe, but he is coming back again in two or three days. I was going to tell you all about our wonderful news, but somehow it isn't the same if you're going away. Shall I ask Uncle Frank to visit you?"

Janet Megan had suddenly become very agitated.

"No, no! I don't want to see him. I shall be gone when he returns. I could not believe it of him! Emma, my dear, I must ask you to go now. I am not feeling quite myself. When I am settled again I will write to you. Goodbye, goodbye!"

She rose to her feet and opened the door for Emma, who walked slowly out, feeling very disappointed indeed. Her visit had not been at all the happy time she had expected.

She had almost reached the bottom of the stairs when the girl with the freckled face appeared again. Emma had never once seen her smile. She looked up at Emma now with quick enquiry.

"Did she tell you?"

"She said she is moving to Overmead."

The girl's eyes narrowed, and her lips were a straight line.

"I knew she wouldn't tell you. She's being turned out; that's why."

"What do you mean?" asked Emma, fearfully.

The girl took her hand, leading her along the passage into a small kitchen.

"I'll tell you what it means. She's being turned out because she didn't pay the rent; leastways, he didn't pay it. He's her brother, and he went off and left her to pay the debt, and she sold all her home up to pay it, and now she's going off somewhere on her own."

Emma was just horrified at this information, and could hardly believe it.

"How do you know all this?" she asked.

"I live here, don't I. Ground floor back. Janet Megan was kind to me, and I wish I could help her. Can't you do something, if you're her friend?"

"Yes. I will do something. I'd better go quickly."

She ran to the front door, and turned back to ask the girl her name.

"Jennifer," said the girl.

Half running, half walking, Emma arrived home much earlier than was expected, out of breath and obviously upset.

Paul met her at the gate.

"What's the hurry, Emma? You do look hot!"

"Where's Daddy? I must see him."

"I think he's in the garden. What's wrong? Can't you tell me?"

But Emma had only one thought in mind.

"I must find Daddy first. I've got something to tell him. Oh, there he is, by the greenhouse."

She ran down the garden, and began to pour out her story in such a rush that her father was quite confused.

"Now, my dear," he said, when he had made her sit down and take a deep breath, "let us begin again, and tell me slowly just what has happened to our friend Janet."

So Emma did her best to give a clear account of what she had seen and heard.

"You will do something, won't you, Daddy," she pleaded. "You will think of something quickly, won't you!"

Her father looked grave.

"Janet Megan is a very independent woman, Emma, but I will do all I can to help her. I only wish I had known about this before. I'll go along to 'Briarcot' and see what plan your mother can suggest."

Comforted and reassured, Emma went in search of Paul. She had boundless confidence in her mother's ability to suggest a plan, and was able to tell Paul about the trouble with a much easier mind.

Mrs. Harris's plan was a simple one. She called on Janet Megan that very afternoon, and begged her to come and help with the pile of sewing and mending that was waiting to be done.

"Emma told me that you were going away," she said, "so I wondered if you could come along and stay with us for a few days before you go. Once you've gone away I shall never get that sewing done, as no one else I know can work as well as you. Lydia is still living at Grandpa's house, so we have plenty of room. I'll come for you in the morning, after breakfast."

"Did she tell you why she was leaving?" enquired John, when his wife returned home.

"No, she told me nothing about her circumstances. The only strange thing was that she seemed anxious to avoid meeting Frank, and I had to assure her that I did not expect him to return for a few days. I thought that she would have been glad to see him, but I suppose she has her reasons for not wishing to meet. Perhaps she doesn't want him to know of her circumstances. She is proud, you know."

Emma was happy to have her friend Janet staying in the house, but she was worried about the future.

"She is only going to stay for two days," she said to Paul, while Janet was sewing busily in the sitting-room. "But what is going to happen to her after that? I wish I was very rich, and could buy her a nice house to live in."

"What puzzles me," remarked Paul, "is why she doesn't want to see Uncle Frank. She always believed he would come back, and she said she loved him. Do you think she owes him some money?"

"Oh, no," said Emma. "He owes her some money."

As soon as the words slipped out Emma remembered that she had promised never to tell anyone that Janet Megan had lent Uncle Frank all her money, and her face went red.

"What money?" asked Paul, quickly. "Why is your face red, Emma? Aren't you telling the truth?"

"Of course I am," she protested; "only I promised not to tell. It just slipped out, that's all. Please don't tell anyone, Paul."

Paul made no reply, but he was thinking deeply. If Uncle Frank had borrowed some money from Janet Megan, he would surely have paid it back. Or if he hadn't returned the money yet, then he certainly intended to do so. Paul could not believe that his uncle Frank was the sort of man who would not pay his debts, especially to friends. It ought not to be a secret.

After tea, when they were all in the sitting-room, talking, Paul kept on looking at Janet with his serious dark eyes full of concern. At last, Janet said quietly:

"What is the matter, Paul? Why do you keep on gazing at me?"

There was a sudden silence, and everyone listened as Paul said, clearly:

"Is it true that you lent Uncle Frank all your money?"

Emma covered her face with her hands; how could Paul give her away like that! How could he be so mean!

Janet asked him in a cold, hard voice who gave him that information.

"Emma didn't mean to tell me," explained Paul. "It only slipped out just this afternoon, so she did keep it a secret for a long time, didn't you, Emma?"

Emma burst into tears. "You are a mean beast, Paul! I asked you not to tell. Daddy is the only one I've ever told, and he knew all about it, but no one else did."

Paul looked from one to the other, and there was an expression on his face that his mother called an 'argumentative air', and he said:

"If Uncle Frank has forgotten to pay back Janet's money, I don't see why it has to be kept a secret."

"Paul," said his uncle John, sternly, "you are talking about things you don't understand. I think you

should apologise to Janet, and go straight up to bed.
I am ashamed of you."

Janet passed a hand wearily across her head.

"Don't scold the boy; he didn't mean to be unkind.
You might as well know the whole story now."

She told them of the night Frank had run away, how
in his sorrow and anger he had gone to her for help, as
he had many times before, in one scrape or another.
He told her that he was one hundred pounds in debt,
and was desperate. It happened that she had just received a legacy of £150, and she lent it all to him. She
even told them that her brother had returned that
same night, and in his anger had pushed her so that
she had fallen on the stairs and hurt her back. She had
not seen or heard of Frank Harris since that night.

The family listened with silent amazement until
Janet had finished; then Isobel Harris asked in a
shocked voice:

"Has he never returned you any of the money?"

Janet shook her head. "No, Frank has never returned one penny of it."

They were all so intent on Janet's story that no one
had heard the car stop in the drive, or noticed the
figure standing in the doorway, and everyone was
startled when a strong voice cried:

"I did return it, Janet. I sent you two hundred
pounds."

At the door stood Uncle Frank, looking straight at
Janet, with absolute honesty written all over his open
face, so that no one could doubt that he was telling
the truth.

White-faced, Janet returned his gaze with equal con-
viction.

"I have never received a penny from you, Frank," she repeated.

Paul looked from one to the other, and wished again that he was a real, grown-up detective, because here was a mystery that must be solved, and solved as quickly as possible.

CHAPTER FIFTEEN

A MYSTERY SOLVED

Now that the secret was out, everybody wanted to ask questions at once, so Uncle Frank sat down and explained very simply what had happened.

"When I left home I really meant to go straight, and return that money before anything else, but a gambling habit is not easily broken. Each time I saved some money, the temptation to double it the easy way was too strong to resist, and it was not until I met Crusoe that I found a better way to live, and even then it took nearly four years to save the money I owed. Then, when I had the hundred pounds, I was faced with a problem. I did not want to send it through a bank, because I did not want anyone to know where I was, and I was afraid to send it by post in case it got lost, so I decided to send it by personal messenger. I knew I could trust Crusoe absolutely, and he promised to deliver it personally, at Miss Megan's address."

"When did you send the money?" asked Janet.

"About three or four weeks ago."

"Then your friend has told you a lie. It was never delivered to me."

Frank Harris jumped to his feet, indignantly defending his friend.

"I will ask Crusoe to tell us himself, now. He is in the breakfast room."

This announcement caused great consternation.

"What! Do you mean you have brought him here,

and left him on his own all this time!" exclaimed Isobel Harris. "Whatever will he think of us!"

"He would not come in until I had asked your permission. He seemed to have some notion that it was not polite, but I will bring him in now. No—Paul, go and fetch Crusoe here, and you will all know that I have not given him any warning."

Paul ran out, and returned with Mr. Crusoe, who was looking very smart in a new suit, and quite handsome, too, with his dark hair carefully brushed back. He bowed, and smiled, as Frank Harris introduced him, and then Frank asked him, quite bluntly:

"Have you ever seen Janet Megan before?"

"No, I have not had that pleasure," he said, gallantly.

"Did you deliver to her a parcel of money?"

Instantly a look of guilt and confusion came over his face.

"The parcel did I deliver, but to this lady, no," he said, finding his words with difficulty, in his agitation.

"Then what did you do with it? Why didn't you tell me this before?" demanded Frank Harris, angrily.

Poor Mr. Crusoe was very distressed.

"I am very sorry. I was frightened of the people. They look at me so—so—what do you say—suspicious. I have been hiding from people, and I think they might recognise me. Might they be informers? Yes? So I give the parcel to the railway man, and he give me his word that he will deliver it. Then I go back to the cabin, quickly."

Poor Uncle Frank groaned and sat down as if his legs suddenly felt weak.

"The railway man! What railway man? He obviously didn't deliver it. What do we do now! Did he steal it?"

Emma, who had been sitting by Janet Megan, sympathetically holding her hand because she was in trouble, was not very quick to grasp the situation, but she did not like to hear a railway man being accused of thieving.

"The ticket-collector at our station wouldn't steal anything. He's our friend, isn't he, Paul!"

"Of course," agreed Paul. "Mr. Jolly wouldn't break his word."

"Old Jolly, is he still there?" exclaimed Uncle Frank. "He was a friend of mine too. We'll go down to the station now. Come on, Crusoe; you'll have a bit of explaining to do."

Paul and Emma pleaded to be allowed to go with him, so they all set off in the car, and a few minutes later drew up at the station.

"Uncle Frank," said Emma, "I remember now; Mr. Jolly told us a foreigner had given him a parcel to deliver, and the man at the house was very cross. I meant to tell Daddy about it, but he was too busy, and then I forgot."

"You may be right, Emma, but we'll soon see. Come along, both of you."

"Wait a minute, please," said Crusoe, and put on a pair of dark glasses, and drew his hair forward, exactly as Paul had seen him do before.

"I said there was only one foreigner," whispered Paul.

Mr. Jolly was astonished to see them. "You could have knocked me down," he said to Emma afterwards, "with a feather from one of my own chickens, I was that flummoxed."

Frank Harris kept in the background, not wishing to confuse Mr. Jolly, while Crusoe and the children stepped forward.

"Mr. Jolly," said Paul, "this is the foreign man we met at Ferry Winton, that I told you about on my post-card. Do you remember him?"

The ticket-collector ran his hand through his stubbly hair, and nodded his head slowly, staring at Mr. Crusoe.

"Yes, I should say it's the same man as wanted a parcel delivered. Mind you, I wouldn't like to swear it in a court of law, there being such cases as twins and doubles, and such, but as far as my memory serves me I should say he is the very same man."

"Mr. Railway Officer," said Crusoe, in great earnestness, "I am the man, as I would swear with my last breath! To you I give the parcel, and you give me your word you will deliver it. I trust you at once; as an English gentleman I trust you, and I go back on the train; and now, you do not deliver it!"

He flung out his arms in a rather wild gesture, and Mr. Jolly drew himself up, and spoke very deliberately.

"When I undertook to deliver that parcel for you, I undertook to deliver it that very day. Coming off duty at 2 p.m. precisely, I went along to feed my hens, as my habit is, and at 2.45 precisely I handed that parcel in to the address as stated. A lot of thanks I got for it, too, as I remember."

"That's right, Mr. Jolly," put in Emma. "You told us the man was as sour as gooseberries, didn't you?"

Mr. Crusoe turned round and beckoned to Frank Harris.

"I told you it was all right," he said.

When Mr. Jolly realised that his other visitor was Frank Harris, his joy and delight knew no bounds, and he shook his hand again and again.

"Young Frank! Well, I can't believe my eyes!"

Paul was pleased and excited too.

"I was coming to tell you all about it, Mr. Jolly," he said, "only we haven't had time since we came back from our holiday."

"Well, I reckon there's a tale to tell, Paul and Emma, so you just come and tell me all about it to-morrow. I was just about to take over when you arrived, and I must get down to the job. But I am real pleased; it's worth more than a mint of money to see you again. I hope there's no trouble about that parcel, but I can assure you that it went to the right house, without a doubt."

As they drove home again, Uncle Frank was very thoughtful, and his face was grave.

"It seems quite clear to me that Janet Megan's brother Ralph took that parcel in, and opened it himself," he said.

Paul's dark eyes were round with astonishment.

"Do you think her brother kept the money himself, and ran away with it?"

Dreadful though the thought was, it proved to be the sad truth. When the circumstances were explained to Janet Megan, she was grieved to the heart. She loved her brother, even though he had been so unkind to her, and she felt the shame of his wrongdoing. He had not only stolen her money, but had left behind large debts that she had sacrificed everything to repay.

When Mr. Crusoe realised what had happened, all because he did not hand the money to Janet personally, he was almost beside himself with regret.

"I beg your pardon, a thousand times," he said to her. "I would rather have the police to find me than bring distress to a lady so sweet. When I am at home again I will send you the money."

Frank wanted to put the matter into the hands of the police, but Janet would not allow this.

"No, please do not inform the police. He is my brother, whatever he has done, and having him imprisoned for theft will only make me more unhappy. Let him go. My one gleam of joy at the moment is that you sent me the money, Frank; you lived up to my trust in you, even if it did take such a long time. That means as much to me as the money itself."

Paul was rather disappointed, as he thought it would be so exciting for the police to chase after Ralph Megan and find him with the money in his pocket, and lock him up in prison.

Emma was inclined to agree with him, as they talked it over before going to bed that night, but she was not so concerned about the culprit being punished.

"I just want Janet to have her money back, and not to have to go away from here, that's all," she said.

CHAPTER SIXTEEN

A HAPPY SOLUTION

Uncle Frank had been at 'Briarcot' for two weeks, and during that time Emma and Paul had learned a great deal about his travels and adventures. Every time Paul thought about the way he had found his uncle, he felt a warm glow of happiness in his heart, not only because it proved he was a good detective, but because his grandfather was so much better since Uncle Frank came home.

Mrs. Appleby said that Grandpa looked ten years younger, and he was 'laying down the law' about the government just like his old self. Mrs. Appleby had been very upset when she heard about Janet Megan's trouble, and had insisted on Janet going to live with her for a few weeks.

"As for that Ralph Megan," she confided to Paul, "what I'd like to do to him I wouldn't like to say. Now there's a case for a detective, Paul—why don't you try to find Janet's brother, and get her money back?"

But Paul shook his head. That was a case for policemen, and Janet didn't want any policemen to find her brother.

Paul talked it over very seriously with his uncle Frank.

"It was your money he ran off with, really, wasn't it! Why don't you try to find him, Uncle Frank?"

"I can't do it, Paul. Janet says perhaps her brother

was in some great need that she knew nothing about, and perhaps if he found out that I was going after him he would do something desperate. What a tender, loving heart that woman has! Ralph Megan doesn't deserve to be loved like that, and forgiven so freely. Come to that," he added, almost under his breath, "none of us deserve to be loved the way we are."

"What do you mean?" asked Paul, whose ears were very sharp.

"Well, look at me, Paul; I ran off full of anger and bitterness, and I have come back to such a loving welcome that I'm sure it is more than I deserve. Then when you think how God loves us, and forgives us, why, it ought to fill our hearts with thankfulness every day of our lives!"

"When did you find out about God, Uncle Frank?"

"Not very long ago, Paul. It was Crusoe who helped me to find Him. I wish I had tried to find Him when I was your age, my lad; I would have saved a lot of people much trouble and sorrow."

A smile lit up Paul's dark eyes, and he took out of his pocket a small text-card, rather crumpled and grubby: 'Seek and ye shall find.' "That's funny," he said. "It was Mr. Crusoe who helped me too, and now I know what this text really means."

"In that case," remarked Uncle Frank, his blue eyes twinkling, "I think we ought to have a celebration. What would you like to do? Shall I conjure up a magic carpet, or hire a coach and six? I can spare a whole day to take you out!"

"And Emma?"

"And Emma, of course! Now, what shall it be?"

"What I would like to do, most of all, is to catch a

train to Overmead, and then change on to the branch
line to Stockton. Mr. Jolly said there's two old engines
there, and the man might let us get up on the foot-
plate. We never, never get a chance to go on the
train!"

"Right! The railway it shall be. Find Emma and
tell her we'll catch the 10.45. Quick's the word!"

Paul ran off, delighted. That was one of the things
he liked so much about his uncle Frank; no sooner did
you think of an idea than, hey-presto! it was put into
action before you could turn round twice, without a
'perhaps' or 'I'll think about it' such as you got from
most other grown-ups.

Emma was happy to go anywhere with Uncle Frank,
and came flying in from the garden as soon as she
heard the news.

"Shall I wear my blue cotton, or my best crimplene,
the pale yellow one?" she wanted to know.

"Definitely not the pale yellow dress for inspecting
railway engines," laughed her uncle, who thought his
young niece looked pretty in anything she wore.

The three of them set off together in high spirits
towards the railway station. They were about halfway
there when Paul heard someone running behind
them. He looked round and saw a girl evidently trying
to catch up with them, so he stood still although he did
not recognise the person.

"Come on, Paul," called Uncle Frank. "We have a
train to catch!"

Then, breathless and panting, the girl caught up
with them, and Emma stared at her with surprise.

"It's Jennifer!" she exclaimed.

It was the thin, freckle-faced girl who lived in the

house where Janet Megan had lived, and she was clutching a long brown envelope.

"Emma," she said, "where is Miss Megan? I've got a letter for her that I found on the mat this morning. It might be important. I knocked at your house and the lady said you were on your way to the station, so I had to run and catch you up."

"She's at Mrs. Appleby's house in Gordan Square. Do you know where that is?"

"I think so. What number is it?"

"I don't remember. Paul, do you remember what number the house is?"

"No, I don't," said Paul, "but she could ask someone in the square. We've got a train to catch."

He looked anxiously towards the station, and thought they might have to start running.

Frank Harris glanced at the envelope, and his face was suddenly grave.

"This might well be very important," he said; "I think I ought to come with you. Sorry, children, but something tells me I ought to follow this up. We'll have to postpone the rail trip."

Paul's heart sank, and his face wore an angry scowl. Bother this girl with her silly letter! Why should she interfere in his special treat! He could feel the quick temper rise up in him, and angry, resentful words came to his lips that would have hurt this girl and his uncle too; but before he could say a word Uncle Frank's hand was upon his shoulder, as though he understood just how Paul felt.

"Come on, Paul," he said, as the girls walked behind them. "A detective often has to forgo his own pleasure when he is on to a clue. You and I might be needed today."

Paul lifted up his head, and his face cleared, as he swallowed his disappointment and tried to think about helping Janet.

"Why do you think that letter is important?" he asked.

"I may be mistaken, Paul, because it is a long time since I last saw Ralph Megan's handwriting, but I think that letter is from him."

Frank Harris's surmise was correct. When Janet Megan opened the letter her face went white.

"Ralph has met with an accident, and is in Westbrook Hospital. The letter is not in his writing, but the envelope is."

"I expect someone found the envelope addressed to you in his pocket, and has written to tell you where he is. Westbrook is only about an hour's run from here. Do you want to see him?"

But poor Janet was so shaken that Frank Harris made another suggestion.

"Let me go and find out just what has happened, Janet. Emma can stay with you, and Paul can come with me. Can you stay, Jennifer?"

"I'd like to," said Jennifer, eagerly.

"Good. You girls can make Janet a nice cup of tea, and I'll send Mrs. Appleby along. Come on, Paul."

It was exciting to be speeding through the countryside again in the small grey car, and reminded Paul of the way they raced home from Ferry Winton when it was thought that Grandpa was dying.

Paul stayed in the car when they reached the hospital while Uncle Frank went to enquire about Ralph Megan. He came back at last, looking very serious.

"We were too late, Paul," he said; "Janet's brother died this morning."

Janet's grief was much lessened when she learned that her brother had written a letter to her, asking for her forgiveness, and returning one hundred pounds of the money he had stolen. She felt that she could lift up her head again, and be happy. But where would she live? The rooms she had rented before were now let to another tenant. But the biggest surprise of all was yet to come.

'Gannet View' the old house at Ferry Winton, was put up for sale, and had already been purchased by a foreign gentleman.

"I wonder who he is?" said Emma, when Uncle Frank had read out this piece of news from a letter he had just received, for the foreign name meant nothing to the listeners.

Uncle Frank burst out laughing.

"You might know the gentleman by his other name, Mr. Crusoe."

"What!" shouted everybody at once.

"Yes, Mr. Crusoe is now the owner of 'Gannet View.' He is a rich man, with far more money than I knew he had, but he has only recently had access to it. He also requests Miss Janet Megan to accept the post of house-keeper, so that when he comes on a visit to England he will always have a place to come to. He thinks perhaps she will have good health in Ferry Winton, which is always dear to his heart. He likes to think the children will have their holidays there, too, and not forget the Mr. Crusoe who found them when they were lost. Well now, what do you think of a plan like that!"

The shouts of delight that greeted this piece of news showed what they all thought of it. Emma begged to be allowed to take the news to Janet Megan straight away, and the surprise and pleasure on Janet's face was beautiful to see.

"Isn't God good to me, Emma," she said. "He has given so many kind friends, and now I shall have a home to live in for the rest of my days. I believe I shall get quite well and strong there too. I am so thankful!"

Even Jennifer shared in the good news, because Janet asked her to spend the first few weeks with her at 'Gannet View', and Paul thought how different Jennifer looked when she was happy, really quite pretty when she smiled. Emma and she were becoming very good friends, and going along to Sunday school together, helping each other to learn the weekly text.

Paul might have felt a bit left out if he had not had some more good news to think about. His father was coming home for good, and they would have their own home again, his mother and father and himself.

"Shall we live in London again?" Paul asked his mother.

"No, dear. I think we'll try to find a house not too far away from Grandpa, so that we can visit him often. Would you like that?"

Paul assured her that he would indeed. When the time came to travel to the airport to meet his father, Paul stood in the big kitchen at 'Briarcot' saying goodbye to his grandfather. He looked thoughtfully round the room, remembering the first time he had seen Uncle Frank's photograph on the dresser shelf.

"Such a lot of things have happened since I came, haven't they, Grandpa?" he said.

Grandpa sat in his big wooden chair, his glasses on the end of his nose, and looked fondly at Paul.

"You certainly started something when you began asking questions about that boy of mine. Are you still going to be a detective, Paul?"

"I am not quite sure, Grandpa," replied Paul. "There's such a lot of things to find out about. I haven't any more lost uncles to find, but Emma says that some people can help to find lost sheep, and bring them back to God. Maybe, when I grow up I'll do that. Perhaps I can do that and be a gardener and a railwayman at the same time. Do you think I can, Grandpa?"

"Sure you can, Paul," smiled Grandpa. "Believe me, a boy can be anything he wants to be, if he makes his mind up, and sticks to it. Now you be off, or you'll be late at the airport."

And as Paul went out, his grandfather uttered a little prayer.

"May the Lord make you a blessing to other people as you have been to your old grandpa." And, smiling contentedly, he settled himself down for his afternoon sleep.